# Where *Are Your* Standards?

## A BOOK FOR WOMEN OF ALL AGES

Real life stories | How to see the truth | Regain your standards

## DEBRA CLIFTON MITCHELL

*Motivational Speaker and Award Winning Author*

LEE'S
PRESS
& PUBLISHING CO.
*"Bringing Content to Life"*

Lee's Press and Publishing Co, LLC

Where Are Your Standards? A Book for Women of All Ages
Real Life Stories, How to See the Truth, Regain Your Standards

Published by Lee's Press and Publishing Company
2618 Battleground Ave
STE A #233
Greensboro NC 27408
www.LeesPress.net

ISBN-13: 978-0-692-69067-3 *Paperback*
ISBN-10: 0692690670

# TABLE OF CONTENTS

Chapter One

# STANDARDS

## *Either you have them or you don't!*

Ladies with standards have more order in their lives- both personally and professionally. Those that don't, have chaos and confusion in every area of their lives. When entering into a relationship, ground rules or standards must be established. If this doesn't occur, you haven't communicated the proper way you are to be treated. This also opens the door to mixed signals, confusion, and miscommunication.

**Most women have three main goals we want to accomplish in our lifetime. It is called the Triple Crown.**

1. To find our dream job or career. This allows us the opportunity to use our skills, talents and abilities and to do work that we find meaningful and fulfilling. It could also include running our own businesses.
2. To find and maintain a healthy and lifelong marriage.
3. To mentor and guide our children to ensure that they are educated, self-confident, gainfully employed, independent and contributing to society.

Somehow, we manage to accomplish two of the three goals quite naturally and quite well. However, when it comes to finding and maintaining healthy and lifelong marriages, we often fall short. I believe this is because many of us don't set standards or more importantly we don't enforce them.

*What are standards?* Well, that depends on who you ask.

This book contains real life stories of women from all walks of life. They come from every age bracket, every income level, and various cultures. I've given them a platform to share their relationship experiences. Most have never had an opportunity and have suffered in silence. Their stories could change or perhaps even save the lives of many women.

What can we do to achieve the third portion of the Triple Crown, the lifelong and healthy marriage? What kind of standards does this require? You must read on for your answer.

Chapter Two
# DATING A MARRIED MAN

*Cassie, age 18 from Kansas City, Kansas*

I was a college freshman away from home for the first time. It was great! I now had the freedom to stay out late and meet people from all backgrounds. Instead of falling for an athlete, I fell for my English professor. He was young, cute and married. This didn't matter to me or to him. He began flirting with me when I went to his office for additional help with my essay. I asked him about his love for the English language. This is when he began reciting words from the play "Romeo and Juliet" by William Shakespeare and the poem "Phenomenal Woman" by Maya Angelou.

I was raised in the Baptist Church and knew better. I knew I had no business flirting with somebody else's husband. Somehow my home training went out of the window. I don't know why – or maybe I do. I am not the prom queen type. I am average in every way. Except academically - this is the one area where I excelled.

Alexander didn't hide the fact that he was married. He told me he got married too young and was very unhappy. That's why he hid in his office instead of going to an unhappy home.

Needless to say, we began sleeping together within two weeks. We would meet at his place when his wife wasn't home or in my dorm room when my roommate was in class. We couldn't be seen on campus so we had to travel at least an hour from campus to low budget hotels. I took the bus, using my limited funds. He didn't even give me bus fare. I felt cheap and guilty, but it wasn't enough to make me stop seeing him. This went on for the whole semester – until I went home for winter break.

I don't know why, but I began telling my friends at home

about Alexander, my new boyfriend, leaving out the fact that he was married. I did the one thing I shouldn't have. I posted a picture of us on social media. My mom warned me about posting things, but I didn't listen. I felt that I was an adult and usually made good decisions.

Alexander and his wife contacted me. I can't repeat what they said to me. My cousin, who was also a professor at the university contacted my mother. He knew Alexander very well. He couldn't believe it and my mom was in shock. I had been an honor student my whole life and never got into trouble.

Alexander got fired and I was too embarrassed to return to school. So I dropped out and got a job at Wal-Mart. My dream of becoming an English Teacher had been put on hold, indefinitely.

### *Sophia, age 38 from Sarasota, Florida*

I had been married to a loser for 15 years and I finally got up the courage to divorce him. I was new to the dating scene. My friends dragged me out to a club one night. I had a few drinks and a few dances with a very handsome man. He didn't have on a wedding ring. I checked, twice!

We exchanged numbers and he was a perfect gentleman. He was everything my loser ex-husband was not. Dabney said all of the right things. He complimented me and showered me with gifts. But there was one catch, he was married with three kids.

Dabney told me he was in the process of moving out so I wasn't too concerned. In my head, I felt he would be divorced soon. We began sleeping together about a week after we met. We had a schedule that we stuck to like clockwork. Dabney put me in his planner and we would meet at a local hotel or my place. As time went by, we started meeting only at my place. There was less chance of us being discovered.

A year went by – it felt like a whirlwind. Then I found out that he never moved out and his wife was pregnant. I was devastated. Then I said to myself "Why should I be devastated"? "She is his wife, not me." I learned a valuable lesson. He is married or he is not, there is no in between. He is now the proud father of four. His wife doesn't even know I existed. I lost a year of my life sleeping with a married man.

### Nadiya, age 31 from Muncie, Indiana

I taught fourth grade at a small school and I loved it. I met Christopher at a parent – teacher conference about five years ago. He was very handsome and I didn't see a wedding ring. I asked him if his wife would be joining us as we discussed his son's progress in school. He said he was married, but not for long.

We discussed his son and my plans for helping him have a successful school year. Afterward, he asked me out. I agreed, thinking he was in the process of divorcing his wife. After quizzing his son, I found out that his dad was still living at home with him and his mother. Even after finding this out, I still kept seeing and sleeping with Christopher. He was telling me to be patient.

A few months later, I found out that I was pregnant. I told Christopher and he had some news for me, his wife was pregnant too. I felt so stupid. How could I allow myself to be in this situation? I am unmarried and pregnant by a married man. I am an educated and independent woman. This is not supposed to be me. Well, reality check, it is me. I come from an upper-middle-class home. My parents have advanced degrees. They were so disappointed in me.

I relocated to Seattle, Washington. I had my daughter three

weeks after his wife gave birth to their daughter. I started teaching again the following year.

My daughter is now three years old. I met and began dating Jacob. He was a great guy. I thought we might have a future together, until I failed "The Mother Test." He took me to meet his mother and she asked about my daughter and her father. I could have lied, but I told her the truth. She said right in front of me "Women who sleep with married men are low class. I think you can do better than her." Jacob dumped me the next week.

### Anastasia, age 19 from St. Cloud, Minnesota

I met Ethan through a mutual friend. At first, I did not know he was married. He laid on the charm. He was handsome and had a good job. While doing a little digging, I found out he was married. When I confronted him, he confirmed he was married, but the marriage was in serious trouble and he was moving out.

We started sleeping together a few weeks after we met. He spent most of his time at my apartment. He started spending nights and weekends. This is why I thought he was telling the truth. Wives don't allow their husbands to be away from home for days at a time. He did one thing that I thought was suspicious. He would run into the bathroom, lock the door and make and receive calls. I never confronted him, even though my gut told me to do so.

I love jewelry and I brought Ethan a chain with a charm on it. One day, while sitting in his car at the park, all hell broke out. His wife Veronica pulled up right next to us. I'm sure she recognized his car and wanted to find out what was going on. She saw the charm I bought him and snatched it off of his neck. She travels a lot on business. This is how he was able to be away from home for days at a time. They got into a physical altercation right there. I jumped out of the car because I thought she might try to jump me next. It was clear that they had fought each other before. I was terrified!

After a few minutes, they stopped and she jumped back in her car calling me a whore and a home wrecker. Ethan was battered and needed medical attention. He was too macho to go to the emergency room. When he got home Veronica had thrown his clothes outside in the front yard and set them on fire. She took their two children and filed for divorce. She also cleaned out his bank account. A week later, he lost his job and his car was repossessed after missing three car payments.

Ethan moved away to Fort Myers Beach, Florida to rebuild his life. He said he would send for me. I thought it would be so exciting to live in sunny Florida. I waited a year for the call, but of course, it never came.

### Keisha, age 33 from Baton Rouge, Louisiana

I met Dennis, age 36 at work. I was a clerk at a gas station. He was a regular customer and always smiled at me and flirted a little. I had just gotten out of a 13-year relationship and wasn't looking for another one.

One day, I was in the store alone. Dennis came in with a single red rose and handed it to me. I smiled and thought this was a really sweet gesture. He admitted that he was married, but he was separated from his wife. She was already living with another man.

We began dating and sleeping together. When I got laid off, I moved into a studio apartment with him and his mother. We slept on the floor and his mother slept in the bed. We would sneak and make love right next to her. This went on for a year and a half. It was exciting at the time. Afterwards, I felt dirty and cheap.

I came to my senses when there was a death in my family. My grandmother passed away. When I went to the funeral, I made the decision to move out. I knew she did not approve of my lifestyle – sleeping on the floor with a married man.

### Jennifer, age 24 from Grand Rapids, Michigan

I met Caleb at work. He was on the IT support team and repaired our computers and installed all of the upgrades. He was very flirty with the girls in the office and didn't wear a wedding ring. However, he seemed to pay more attention to me.

He asked me out to lunch with him one day. Of course, I agreed. This became a standing date. Every Friday, we would meet at our local spot. One day, when we were returning from lunch, one of my girlfriends pulled me to the side. She whispered in my ear, "Caleb is married. I just wanted you to know." I sat there stone faced and didn't know what to do. We were emotionally connected. I was young and naïve at the time and didn't ask Caleb about his marital status. I guess I didn't want to hear the answer.

Caleb was also a musician, he played the drums at several clubs around town. He would ask me to come out to hear the band on Fridays. He would leave a ticket for me at the door. By this time, we had been kissing and touching on each other, but we hadn't slept together – yet. We both knew it was coming.

After about 3 months, we made plans to spend the night together after we left the club. He left my ticket at the door to sit in the VIP section. I was going to take the train downtown and our magical night would begin. Boy, was I was dressed for the occasion. I had on a tight leather mini-skirt, fishnet stockings, a black and red bustier, 5 inch spiked heels and a long, black coat.

On my way to catch the train, I tripped and broke my toe. I had to be rushed to the emergency room. When I got there all of the triage nurses stared at me. I really looked like a hooker. Then I said to myself "What are you doing"? "You are better than this."

I believe it was divine intervention. God stopped me and saved me from myself. Every time I look at my toe, it is a constant reminder about my bad choice. My toe did not heal properly and to this day, I can't wear heels.

Caleb stopped speaking to me because I stood him up. All he wanted from me was sex. I saw him flirting with a girl on the next floor. I should have warned her that he is married. However, I decided to keep my mouth shut.

### Margaret, age 38 from San Antonio, Texas

Noah worked at the Sanitation Department in town with me. It was no secret that he was married. This was a very dark period in my life. I started drinking heavily due to a bad breakup. We became physical after about one month of meeting.

To make matters worse, he had been sleeping with Sarah, another girl in my department. Everybody was always whispering about them. We went to lunch and sometimes to a hotel during lunch. He was a steady blue collar worker and didn't dress up or live an exciting life. The only thing he was good at was sex. He said he was going to leave his wife.

Noah told me he wanted to marry me. There was only one problem – I was not in love with him. He was a simple, country boy. He had a good heart, but he was not the one for me. By the time his divorce was final, I had moved on. He went from three

9

women to none in a matter of months.

### *Raquel age 15 from Greenville, South Carolina*

I met Aaron when I was in the eighth grade. He lived around the corner with his wife and family. He was 20 years older, age 35. We started dating when I was in high school. I was very mature for my age and I knew from day one that he was married. As a matter of fact, he had a daughter the same age as me.

He took me to some exciting places and showered me with gifts. He always gave me money and I always felt special around him. This was not a fling. I felt he was MY man. At age 21, I got pregnant with a daughter. At first, he was involved in her life, then all of that changed. When my daughter was three years old, his wife found out about us. Her sister discovered our affair and found out about our daughter. We never went around in secret, so I guess I was surprised it took us so long to be discovered. As I said, in my mind, he was my man.

As time went on, I felt cheated. I felt that Aaron had robbed me of my youth. He had no intention of leaving his wife. I guess I never expected him to. He paid me money for child support, but it wasn't consistent. My mother encouraged me to take him to court to pay child support every month. Then he did what all the men that cheat do, he said my daughter was not his. So off to court we go. We had a DNA test performed and he was the father. He began paying child support, however, he refused to be in our daughters' life.

She is hurt and bitter and has suffered in her own relationships. She recently announced she is bi-sexual. I think some of this has to do with her lack of a father figure. She has a low view of men.

Aaron's wife stayed with him after she found out about us, they are still married today.

# How To See The Truth

Marriage includes words such as commitment, exclusive and wedlock. Wedlock means locking out all others – and that means you. The truth is – you are not his wife. You are wasting your valuable time with someone else's husband.

Married men are master manipulators. They lie to you and their wives on a constant basis. You don't even know if you are his only sidepiece. You could be one of many "other" women. They tell you how unhappy they are at home. Most importantly, they give you, at least, a dozen reasons why they are not divorced. They know what words to say to make you feel special. There is one catch, this is only temporary. These men return home to their wives and family and act as if you don't exist. They are also very greedy. They want the wife, children and the American dream and they want the excitement of an affair.

**They keep you in a box and they keep the key. They do all of the following:**

- Tell you when to call – cell number only. He probably  bought the phone for you so he can keep track of your calls.
- Tell you where to meet, often outside of town and many times after dark.
- Tell you that you can't visit at his home or meet any members of his family.
- He may tell you the whole family is deceased. This is a complete lie. Everybody is related to somebody. You may be dating both a con-man and a married man.
- Tell you that he can't see you on his birthday or on holidays.

- Tell you that they are going to leave their wives, but you never see any evidence of this.

My grandmother told me when I was a teenager "Never give your good years to a bad man." Dating a married man is bad for you on so many levels. The truth is most married men never leave their wives.

# Regain Your Standards

Why are you letting someone control you by putting you in a box? This is America the land of the free and you are over the age of 18. You are dating below standards if you are dating someone else's husband. Stop sharing your time, your body and your resources with him. You can't compete for him, she's already won. Remember, she's the wife.

**You need to bow out gracefully. Get out of the box he put you in. Here's your exit strategy.**

- Stop taking his calls
- Change your number.
- Refuse to see him.
- Don't try to collect anything from him or return anything to him. It's over.
- Don't accept any gifts from him

**Now that you are out of this bad relationship, here's how you can avoid getting into it again in the future.**

- When you meet a man for the first time, ask him if he is married. If he is, move on. Don't even give him your number.

- Realize some men are not going to be truthful upfront, do your own detective work. If you find out he's married, drop him and don't look back.
- The same rules apply if he lives with his girlfriend.

In a few rare instances, a man leaves his wife and marries his girlfriend. And what does he do? He cheats on her too! A marriage born out of an affair is doomed to fail. He hasn't changed his behavior, he just changed his wife.

## *Where Are Your Standards?*

## Chapter Three
# DATING OR MARRYING AN EX-CON

*MacKenzie, age 42 from Chicago, Illinois*

I met John, age 40, about five years after he was released from prison. He was in a shelter and I work in social services. He was a part-time cook at a local restaurant. He said it was just too boring for him and soon quit. I asked him about his past. He grew up in Jackson, Mississippi and moved here when his grandmother passed away. He never graduated from high school and got into trouble soon after he moved here. I guess he got in with the wrong crowd. He had been arrested for armed robbery, assault and battery and drug trafficking.

I am one of those women who loves the underdog. I honestly thought I could change him. I had a vision of helping him get his G.E.D. and a full-time job. After 3 months, he moved in with me. I thought he was listening as I explained about the importance of completing his High School Equivalency Exams and some job for ex-cons with their G.E.D. I pushed and pushed for him to complete his G.E.D. I purchased all of the books and study materials for him and also prepared a study guide for him.

I have four kids, two are still in high school and they were studying the same material. I thought this would be easier for him. I often had study sessions with my children over the years, so one more "student" was no problem for me. However, this turned out to be a huge problem for him. He resented any help from me or my kids. He didn't want to help out around the house when I asked him to do small things like take out the garbage or cut the grass. Simple things he could be doing when he was not studying.

When it came time for him to take his exams, he never

showed up. He just blew them off. They offered a make-up session, in case of emergencies. Well, he blew them off too! My son, age 16, asked me why he was having such a hard time understanding simple algebra. Of course, I made excuses for him. After all, he was 40 years old and had not had any formal education in over 20 years.

I later found out, he dropped out of school in the 7th grade. I have a Master's Degree in Social Work. I am not arrogant and don't have a sense of superiority. I really didn't expect him to go to college, but I did expect him to get his G.E.D. and a full-time job. I also found out that he was still hanging out with some other ex-cons when he was supposed to be looking for work. My gut told me he was still doing something illegal, but I ignored it.

My daughter, age 20 came over one day and asked if we were getting married. She asked me this right in front of John. John immediately said "yes" and I was surprised. I hesitated and knew it was against my better judgment, but two weeks later, we got married at the courthouse.

One week before our first anniversary, I filed for divorce. John never took the test for his G.E.D and never looked for work. I was able to get him odd jobs around the neighborhood, but he quit every one of them after two days.

John was not the man of the house in any way, shape or form. My 16-year-old was more mature and responsible than he was, even he had a part time job after school. We packed up his things and took him back to the shelter where I met him. In retrospect, I guess finding a husband in a shelter is not the smartest thing I have ever done.

### Brooke, age 42 from Roanoke, Virginia

Eli, age 44, was an ex-con from Columbus, Georgia. He moved to Roanoke after serving 3 years for shoplifting or "boosting" and stealing cars for his drug habit. He found a job as a telemarketer because they don't do background checks.

He had been out about a year when I met him. We met at a restaurant. I was having dinner with some of my friends and he gave me his number. We dated for about 2 months before I let him move into my apartment. I worked at a bank as a teller.

Life was good for him; he gave me his whole check. I controlled all of the money. He stopped smoking, drinking and using drugs while we were together. He really transformed and was happy. He said I was his motivation and he didn't want to disappoint me.

Life wasn't so good for me. He begged and begged me to marry him. I refused. I didn't want to be his crutch and felt he should lead a clean and sober life on his own. Then he lost his job. He looked for work, but it is very hard for an ex-con to find a job. We filled out a bunch of applications, but all were doing background checks. I didn't want to be on that roller coaster with him of highs and lows. I predicted mostly lows because of his inability to find and keep a job. I kicked him out of my apartment after another marriage proposal. I felt it was too much pressure for me.

I heard he is back on drugs and back in jail.

### Ella, age 18 from Bayonne, New Jersey

Demetrius had served time for drugs and gun possession. He had a cherry, red Buick Park Avenue and all the girls noticed it. It was a real chick magnet. I was walking home one day and he pulled over and started flirting with me through the window. I already knew his family because my best friend previously dated his brother. Demetrius came from a dysfunctional family. His mother made him and his brothers physically fight against each other. All three of them had been in jail at one time or another.

We had been dating for about two months when I found myself in the middle of two shootouts. It is only by the grace of God that I didn't get hit. I decided it was time to break up. He became very possessive and said to me "You can't leave me" again and again. I felt trapped.

Things really got bad about a month later when he came by my house making a huge commotion. He was screaming my name at the top of his lungs and demanding that I come outside. I ran to the front porch because I certainly did not want him to come inside my house. He grabbed me and threw me in his car. His friend was driving. I started screaming at him and reminding him that this was kidnapping. He screamed at his friend to pull off. He wouldn't do it. He was able to calm him down and I was able to get out of the car. I don't know why, but I continued to see him.

This relationship ended when he stole my car. That was my breaking point. He is back in jail. This time, he's serving time for grand theft auto.

### Daniyah, age 27 from Charlotte, North Carolina

I met Isaac at an Alcoholics Anonymous (AA) meeting. I had been clean and sober for eight years. My sponsor told me not to date him because he was just beginning his recovery. He was recently released from prison and was trying to get his life on track. He had done time for assault and battery against three women. She told me I would be raping him if I didn't give him a chance to become strong, clean and sober like me.

Well, I ignored all of that. I moved Isaac into my apartment two weeks later. We were intimate almost every day. He was a perfect maid. He cleaned and ironed all of my clothes. The apartment was spotless. He was good with my son who was four years old at the time.

I was good for him. I made sure he got to his AA meetings and I thought I could change him. I even helped him get a job at a car wash. He made $300 a week and he gave it all to me. He complained about his back and knees hurting. He started missing days and then he just stopped going to work. Eventually, they fired him.

Isaac had emotional problems and started drinking again. He told me it was easier to be back on the inside. At least, he had three meals and a clean bed and no one expected anything from him. I had too many rules for him on the outside. He wrecked my car and stole money from my son's piggy bank, that's when I called the police. When he was arrested, I found out he had an outstanding warrant. He's back in prison, this is the fourth time he's been incarcerated.

### Charmaine, age 28 from New Haven, Connecticut

I met Sean, age 32 at church. He was a new member. I grew up in church and thought it would be a good place to try to find a husband. We met at Vacation Bible School and taught classes on the same floor. We hit it off and started dating. I was trying to get my life together; I have three children by three different men. Two were born out of wedlock and one by my ex-husband. Sean said his wife was deceased and he had three girls. He is also an ex-Marine.

While we were dating, I noticed he was going back and forth to court a lot. Since I just met him, I didn't inquire. I just assumed he was handling some military business. He was kind and attentive and took good care of his daughters.

We got married after dating for a year and a half. He was raised by his older sister, Doreen, his mom died when he was a child. She and I never got along. I really don't know why. She was very evasive and cold towards me. About a year after we got married, Doreen and I had a serious disagreement. I was so upset, I called Sean and found out she had too. She requested a family meeting to help clear the air.

At the meeting, she made Sean come clean. I sat there with a puzzled look on my face. Sean had been out on parole when I met him at church. He had been charged with killing his wife. He shot her to death. Oh My God! This explains why he was always going back and forth to court.

I had no idea I was married to a murderer! Of course, he claims it was an accidental shooting. Either way, I felt like I was sleeping with the enemy and I could be next. How did I know he wouldn't kill again? By this time, I was three months pregnant with my fourth child. Sean struck a plea deal and he was sentenced to ten years in prison. I can't believe that he didn't tell me that he killed his wife. I would never have married him nor had a child with him. My whole world came crashing down around me and I went into a deep depression.

After my son was born, I decided to forgive him. For five years, I took my four kids to see him. I got tired of hauling them for the three hour drive to prison and explaining why he couldn't come home with us. I really struggled to pay my bills. He, of course, wasn't able to provide any support because he was incarcerated. I was collecting child support from the other men, but it wasn't consistent.

By now, I was 33 years old and had found a job as an office manager for Adam, a chiropractor in town. Adam was married with three kids. He was a good listener and I shared with him that I had four kids and my husband was in jail. To say, I was not interested in any man at this point in my life, would be a huge understatement.

Adam was very caring. He even bought me a car so I could get around better with my four kids. I think I was a "sympathy case" for him. A few months after Sean was incarcerated, a man broke into my apartment and sexually assaulted me. I was broken, sad and alone. Adam became my protector.

I worked hard for him and helped him grow his business. Sometimes we had to double book the clients and his business was booming. We were great business partners and I loved my job. After two years, I made a fatal mistake. I started sleeping with my boss, the married man. We were careless and I became pregnant, with my now fifth child by five different fathers.

My daughter was born while I was still married to Sean. When I told him, he blamed himself for not being there for me. He said he knew I was lonely and he forgave me for cheating on him. I divorced him while he was still incarcerated. Adam never left his wife, but he does pay child support.

### Sabrina age 22 from, Bismarck, North Dakota

I met Scott while I was bartending. He worked for a muffler and tire shop. I fell head over heels for him. He had red hair, blue eyes, nice body...just totally good looking! We dated for about three years and unexpectedly, I found out I was pregnant. Instead of rejoicing with me, he claimed he wasn't the father. He swore to me he had a vasectomy. I thought that was strange because he was only 28 years old. Since I was a bartender, he assumed one of the regulars at the bar was the father.

My son was born the following August. We had a DNA test done, Scott is the dad. The test showed 99.99 percent. Scott Junior (SJ) looks just like him. He was involved with him from the start.

Scott and I got along for the most part. I did have to deal with his bad temper. He was not the jealous type, but he did have one serious problem. He was in and out of prison for a variety of offenses, one of which was driving without a license.

He had become a Habitual Offender. This means he had three unrelated felonies and he faced significant additional prison time if caught again. He could be charged with an additional six to twenty years.

One morning, he called to tell me he dropped SJ off at school, which was only a block away. He was five years old. I said "Good, Don't be driving anywhere else." He said he knew better. We were laughing and cutting up because January 8th is Elvis Presley's birthday and I told him we should be down at Graceland! He got a kick out of that. That was about 9:30 a.m. I sent a funny text and a joke, but didn't get a response. I figured he was asleep or something. About 11:15 a.m. my dad called and asked if I had heard from him. I said "Yea, about 9:30 a.m." My dad already knew something tragic had occurred. He was listening to the police scanner. My dad had to tell me the most haunting, dark news that I have ever experienced. Scott had committed suicide. He shot himself in the mouth with a 9mm. I have never in my life been as hurt as I was that day.

He was out driving and a local police officer got behind him and flipped on the flashing lights. He swerved the jeep to the left of the curb and shot himself. He always said he would NEVER go back to prison and he ended his own life.

My mom went to pick up SJ from school and he was asking "Where is my dad? Why didn't he pick me up?" We all gathered at my grandmother's house and my uncle told SJ in a spiritual way that his dad had taken his life. At five years old, it didn't make sense to him. We had to console him and assure him that his dad loved him. Until this day, he sometimes asks me what happened to him. He is now 11 years old and we just can't tell him the truth, both of us have gone through grief counseling in order to cope with all of this.

I had a chance to speak to the Police Detective and I asked how much time Scott would have faced since he was caught driving again without a drivers' license. I knew he was a felon. He told me he would have gotten ten years for driving as a Habitual Offender and another ten years for having a gun with no permit. I just wished he would have chosen a different way and not done this to my son and I.

### Lorraine, age 25 from Naperville, Illinois

I met Jeffrey at age 17. I grew up in a very strict home. No makeup, no cell phone and definitely no dating. I couldn't even participate in any after school activities. My life was so boring. I couldn't wait until I turned 18 to get out of there.

Jeffrey was 19 and was a typical bad boy. He dropped out of high school in his senior year. I was a junior when we met in Biology class. I knew he was a trouble maker and wasn't surprised when he dropped out. He just stopped coming to school and had fallen too far behind to ever catch up.

Right after dropping out, he beat up an old lady and stole her purse. He also had a lot of petty theft charges against him. It got so bad that one store on the corner of my block put up his picture in the window with a warning not to enter the premises again. He was no longer welcome because he stole them blind every time he entered the store.

I ran into him about a month later. I was coming out of a grocery store and he helped me with my bags. What I didn't realize was that he had just stolen items from there and was using me as a decoy. We exchanged numbers and started dating. I started skipping school so I could be with him. Within two weeks, we were sleeping together. He was my first and I thought we would be together forever.

Three months later, I turned 18. I knew I wasn't required to attend class and there was nothing my parents could do about it. Jeffrey and I spent all day together and I wasn't on birth control. I never thought about asking him to use a condom. I left home at the same time every morning so no one had any idea I wasn't in school. When I missed my period, I knew right away that I was pregnant. I told Jeffrey and we were both very excited. I decided to move in with him and drop out of school. He was the maintenance man at a large apartment complex and had a free apartment in the basement. When I told my parents, they stopped speaking to me. I only had a few months until graduation.

I got a job at Walgreens before I started showing. Jeffrey got a job at McDonalds working at night. We started saving for the baby and I thought everything was great. Our daughter, Veronica was born eight months later. When she was a month old, all of our savings was gone. We miscalculated the cost of having a baby. I didn't have a baby shower because I was estranged from my family and all of my friends thought I was bad news. My former best friend told me her mother called me a tramp and idiot for dropping out of school in our senior year. Before I met Jeffrey, we talked about being roommates in college. She had gotten accepted to Illinois State University and I didn't even finish my college applications.

When Veronica was about six months old, Jeffrey started stealing on a regular basis. He started with the residents of the apartment complex. He stole items he could pawn while they were at work. He had the master key and had gained the trust of the residents and the owner of the building. He took items like cell phones, tablets, laptops, jewelry and small flat screen televisions.

I don't know what he did with the money because he never bought anything for Veronica and me. Two months later, he got fired because he was caught on camera with some of the stolen items. He didn't know one of the residents had suspected him and set up a hidden camera in his unit. Jeffrey had two bags of stolen items including some steaks that he stole from the refrigerator. I guess he was hungry and ate them because we never had any steak dinners. After we got evicted, we moved into a low budget motel and paid rent by the week.

For about 4 months, we really struggled. That's when Jeffrey came up with his "get rich quick" scheme. We were going to steal from the Walgreen's store that I worked at. He told me to go to work and fill up the baskets full of items we really needed. Things like baby supplies, food, soap, toothpaste and deodorant.

At first, I refused to even entertain such an idea. However, after another month of drinking water for breakfast, lunch and dinner, I had a change of heart. I lost so much weight and had constant headaches. Also, I had no energy and I knew I couldn't go much longer without any food. I only fed our daughter.

I knew what time all of the managers would be gone and I arranged the whole thing. I switched my hours to make sure that only a couple of people would be there. They worked in the stockroom. I loaded up 3 baskets full of stuff I wanted.

Jeffrey came in and I showed him where the baskets were. He condensed them into two baskets that were overflowing. Then he walked right out of the door, ignoring the buzzer, like most customers. The raggedy car we had was parked around the corner. One of his friends helped him load the car. I went into the back and acted like I didn't know what was going on. I started helping them stock the items because we didn't have any customers. This was a satellite store with very little traffic after 8:00 p.m. That evening, the cupboards were full of things like oatmeal, cereal, milk, juice and my baby had diapers and supplies. I thought we got away with it until that terrible day.

About two weeks later, I was at work when the police came in the store. My manager asked that I come to his office in the back. The police officer told me I was under arrest for theft. My manager asked for my employee I.D. and I was fired on the spot. They took me to the police station in the squad car. I was so embarrassed and ashamed of myself.

When I got to the police station, I confessed everything. I was charged with shoplifting and to pay $5000 in restitution and several fines. I also got three years of probation. I didn't call Jeffrey to tell him what happened. I called my parents and begged them to let me come home. They only let me in because of Veronica. My mom told me," It's not her fault she has you as a mother. I can't believe you did something like this". "You are supposed to be her role model. Is this what you want her to grow up to do?" These words cut like a knife. This was my wake up call.

That was 5 years ago. I haven't seen Jeffrey and he is not

involved in Veronica's life. He is incarcerated. He's been in and out of jail so many times, I have lost count. I don't know all of the charges and I really don't care. Even though the probation period is up, I am still struggling to pay the fines and restitution. I went back to school and got my G.E.D. and I thought my past was buried. I applied for a job as a customer service rep at a prestigious bank. I completed the phone interview and really impressed them during my interview in person. A few days later, the H.R. person called and told me I had the job.

The following Monday, I started my orientation and was making new friends. We were told to bring some pictures and other items to make our workstation more comfortable. On Tuesday, I returned with my items to decorate my workstation. After lunch, I got a call to report to H.R. I thought it was to pick up my employee I.D. with the picture I had taken the day before. They told me I failed the background check due to my shoplifting charge and I was fired. My new career ended as soon as it started.

I am a common criminal and so ashamed. I feel like my life is over at age 25. If I didn't have Veronica, I wouldn't keep trying. I'm now trying to find an attorney that will help me get my record expunged. I'm working at a bar because they didn't do background checks. I don't know how many years it will take me to recover from all of this.

# How To See The Truth

I first want to express my condolences to Sabrina and SJ and their families. Dealing with death is hard enough at any age. However, dealing with a suicide adds another layer to the grief process. I'm glad to hear that both of them had counseling to be able to cope with this terrible loss.

Committing suicide is an act done when the person doesn't have the ability to think about those that love them. I'm certain Scott loved both Sabrina and their son, but facing a lengthy prison sentence overpowered him and he made that fatal decision.

The truth is, ex-cons come with a lot of baggage. They have a problem living within the law. They think the laws don't apply to them. That is until they get caught. This is why they are now convicted criminals with a record. Most of them are repeat offenders and have trouble living among law abiding citizens.

The truth is he will have a difficult time finding a job or a career. If he finds a job, it will probably be a minimum wage, dead-end job. He will probably become bored and quit. Therefore, jumping from job to job. This appears to potential employers as a person who is unstable. Eventually, he will be unemployable.

The truth is you will wind up supporting a grown, able bodied man because of his poor choices, not yours.

# Regain Your Standards

You are now supporting a grown, able bodied man. Are you o.k. with this? Why? I'm sure he told you that you can't do any better. Do you believe this? Well, it is not true!

What attracted you to him? How did your two worlds meet?

Do you date ex-cons on a regular basis? If so, why?

Are you a person who thinks you can change him? Are you a person who thinks you can fix him? Are you a person who thinks you can cure him? The only person you can change is yourself. Understand and accept this today!

The good news is that there are several programs available to ex-cons to help them become productive citizens. However, it is not the job of a girlfriend or wife to help them complete these programs. They have to be motivated and disciplined enough to find these programs themselves and take control of their futures. Don't wait for him to get his life together. Date other people who you are interested in. It may take years for him to improve. Some good signs are:

- He obtained a job and has kept it without incident for at least a year.
- He has his own apartment and is paying all of the utilities and rent with no assistance.
- He has not become a repeat offender.

If you are married to an ex-con, do you respect him as the head of the household? Respect is a feeling of deep admiration for someone. Does he support the family, both financially and emotionally? Do you consider him a role model for the children? Is he working hard to ensure the success of the family? Is this marriage working for you now and for the long haul? Do you want your children to grow up and marry ex-cons? Remember, you are your child's first and best teacher.

# Where Are Your Standards For Your Family?

Chapter Four

# DATING OR MARRYING A LAZY, UNMOTIVATED MAN

## *Zoe, age 40 from Columbus, Ohio*

We got married at age 23. My husband Xavier is only two months older than me. I finished college and took a job at an insurance company as an underwriter. Xavier dropped out with a promise to return to college. We were young and in love and I agreed to handle the financial responsibilities of the family. We rented a house while he was supposed to pursue his degree in Chemistry. However, after 17 years of marriage, he still had no full-time, steady job and no college degree.

He was a house husband and took classes here and there, but with no direction or proof that he was a degree-seeking student. He got jobs in the same fashion. He worked in clerical jobs, landscaping, plumbing and whatever else. But nothing amounted to anything. He didn't even earn enough to file taxes each year. In the meantime, I was getting promoted and doing very well in corporate America.

I expected our roles to change when I got pregnant with our first daughter. Well, that day never came. He never changed, not even a little. I saw no signs of improvement. We now have three daughters, they are honor students and on their way to college. He is still lazy and unmotivated to find a steady job with benefits.

One day, my oldest daughter asked him if he had a career. He couldn't answer her. At that time, he was shoveling snow for the neighbors and told her he had a snow blowing business, but didn't even own a snow blower. Then she asked me a question.

She said with those beautiful brown eyes, "Mom, should I marry a man like dad?" I asked her what kind of man she think her dad is. She used the same words "lazy" and" unmotivated". "He does the bare minimum so you don't kick him out." Well, I kicked him out because I want my daughters to do better than me. It's funny how it took this conversation to wake me up. I felt so stupid and used. We divorced three months later.

### Wanda, age 51 from Madison, Wisconsin

We had a good marriage for 21 years, then Eugene lost his job. He wouldn't tell me what happened. To this day, I don't know if he got fired or got laid off. What I do know is 10 years went by and he refused to find a full-time job with benefits.

We have five kids and three were still at home. I began part-time work while raising the children. I did so well, that I was offered a full-time job. However, it wasn't enough to cover the mortgage, the children's expenses and all of the household bills.

I complained and complained for 10 years. I thought he would change. The little money he collected from unemployment didn't put a dent in our bills. I wanted him to return to work and get a full-time job and help keep the family afloat. Eugene has a college degree in Finance, but instead of returning to his field, he took a job as a camp counselor. It was part-time and seasonal.

You can't support a wife and kids with a part-time camp counselor job. This was a job for a high school or college student not a 50-year-old man. I think I would have stayed if he would have gotten a decent job and provided for us. Well, we lost everything. I moved in with my elderly parents. My marriage was over.

## Julie age 49 Buffalo, New York

I met Carlos at a church function. Unfortunately, I have not had much success in the romance department. I have three failed marriages and five children, all now adults. I am a hopeless romantic and couldn't fathom living the rest of my life alone.

Carlos, age 50 was a gentleman and also once divorced. We dated for a few months and got serious pretty fast. Carlos was very good looking. He would be classified as a "Pretty Boy." During our courtship, he expressed he wanted to settle down with a good woman for good. His divorce was very painful and so was mine.

As we began dating, I noticed something that I didn't like. He was used to women taking care of him, not the other way around. You see, I'm from the old school and expect the man to take care of his woman. Within a few months, we were engaged. I ignored the signs that he would be problematic. I don't know why. I guess I liked the feeling of falling in love with a new man. Anyway, I started to feel nervous and anxious about marrying him. So I called off the wedding. I knew this was a sign from God.

Carlos begged me to marry him. I broke down and went through with it. Once we were married, I saw the same signs again. He wanted me to support him and provide for him. He really didn't work consistently. He always claimed he was broke and made excuses for not paying the bills. He showed no motivation to make ends meet every month.

All of his previous relationships involved women who catered to him. He wasn't ready for me. You see, I am a strong, independent woman and not interested in supporting a man. After a few months, I left him and thought about divorce.

Carlos agreed to go to counseling with me to save our

32

marriage. He told me how lonely he was when I was gone and now understood what was required of him as my husband. After six months, I returned home. We are working on our marriage and there has been one major change. He is responsible for all of the monthly household bills! This is the bare minimum that I expect as his wife. I demand to be treated like a lady!

I think the reason I had so many failed marriages is because I didn't demand that they step up to the plate and be the man of the house. I won't make that mistake again! For me, the fourth time is the charm.

# How To See The Truth

This man is struggling with low self-esteem. Yes, men have it too! He has low expectations for himself. He's probably been told all of his life that he will never amount to anything. The sad thing is, he actually believes it. This is why he doesn't even try to do any better.

The truth is he has no goals for himself. These types of people are just existing in the world. This is why he is lazy and unmotivated. I wouldn't be surprised if everything he has was given to him. Someone probably gave him a job as a favor to you or his mother. Somebody probably gave him an old, raggedy car. He is gainfully employed and can be counted on for a paycheck, even if it is part-time or seasonal. This is a positive thing. However, the truth is, he is in his comfort zone and has no intentions of leaving.

# Regain Your Standards

This lifestyle works for him. This is why he is unmotivated to change it. At least, he has a job and the basics; food, clothing and shelter. Here are a few questions for you. Is he living up to his full potential? Does he complain about not having the things he wants, but doesn't do anything about it? If you are dating, can he afford to live on his own or is he required to live with family or friends? Is this standard acceptable to you? If so, what kind of future do you see with him? If you are married, do you argue about paying the monthly expenses? Do you have any savings? Or maybe you are both the same. Are you lazy and unmotivated too? If so, maybe you two are a perfect match. Most people marry people that they have things in common with.

If not, is this the life you envisioned? What are you going to do to change it? The only way to regain your standards is to stop living in denial and determine if this is the life you want.

Motivation is internal. You can't give it to another person. He has to get motivated on his own. Are you going to wait for this to happen? If so, how long? One year, five years or ten years?

Accept the fact today that the only person you can change is yourself. If you decide to wait and hope for the best, please remember you can't get those years back. A man is designed to complement a woman, not complete her. We are whole with or without a man.

Establish goals and strategies to reach them. If he's on board, great! If not, now that you see the truth, it's time to set some new standards for your family. Remember, your children are watching you and depending on you. Your standards affect them too. They may never be motivated to leave home and the vicious cycle will continue. It's up to you to break it.

## Where Are Your Standards?

## Chapter Five

# DATING OR MARRYING A CONTROL FREAK

### *Isabella, age 29 from San Diego, California*

I married into money and along with it came my control freak husband, Larry. I grew up in an affluent family. I attended private schools and graduated from college with no student loans. During my sophomore year, I studied abroad.

 My father told me that young ladies get their wealth in one of two ways, we either marry into it or inherit it. He said he was too young to die, so I might as well get married.

My wedding was simply beautiful. It looked like something right out of a magazine. We had the ceremony at a local country club. I was 24 and Larry was 34. He came from one of the wealthiest families in the area. Since he was ten years older, he was already established as a financial advisor and worked at his father's firm. We moved into our home shortly after the wedding, which was valued at $850,000 with six bedrooms. He said this was our starter home.

Life was wonderful in the beginning. He let me furnish the house my way. I must say that I have exquisite taste, with a millionaire husband, money was no object. I also enjoy artwork and purchased many famous pieces and the house looked like a show place. Larry, on the other hand, loved jewelry and he showered me with diamonds, pearls, sapphires, and gold.

If this sounds like a fairy tale, believe me, it was not. The fun stopped after I finished decorating the house. Even though I married a millionaire, I was given a debit card with a limit of $1000.00. Larry told me not to use it because he had already provided anything and everything I wanted. I felt like a bird locked in a cage.

He gave me a cell phone and told me I could only use it once a week to call my mother. He checked the phone activity daily, just to make sure. Our conversation had to last 10 minutes or less. Also, I had to wait for him to come home so he could listen to our conversation. I couldn't talk about our marriage and always had to say everything was fine.

In addition to all of this, I had to cut ties with all of my childhood and college friends. I couldn't even attend a homecoming game sponsored by my sorority. He called my friends trash and told me I didn't need them or anybody for that matter. He told me what to eat and we were only intimate if he put it on the calendar. I had to participate whether I wanted to or not. Once I said I had a headache and he raped me and told me to take an aspirin later.

After about two years of this, I knew I had made a big mistake, but I thought I would try to salvage my marriage. I went shopping for some new underwear without his knowledge. I brought a bra that allowed me to show some cleavage in the black dress I bought myself for my birthday. I planned to wear it to dinner with him. He hit the roof and exploded. You would think I told him I became a stripper or something like that. I was only 25 and still had a cute figure and wanted to show it. He got so mad he cut up my dress and my debit card. He said I needed to be "supervised" while I shopped. This is when I began my exit plan.

On our third anniversary, I called him and asked him to meet me at his favorite restaurant at a fancy hotel downtown. He had gone shopping with me several times and I had a closet full of "appropriate" dresses that looked more like my grandmother's suits when she went to a funeral.

Instead, I moved out all of the furniture, artwork and jewelry and put it in storage. Then I moved in with my two brothers, both of which absolutely hated him. I never showed up at the restaurant. Instead, I told the process server where to find him and they delivered the divorce papers to him. He told me Larry flipped out and knocked over the table breaking several dishes. Of course, he threw a few thousand dollars at them and they looked the other way. This is another sign of a control freak. They think their money can fix anything.

Six months later I was divorced. I knew I had to stand up for myself and stop being treated like a five-year-old. I made Larry pay all of my legal fees and I got a significant divorce settlement because we did not sign a pre-nuptial agreement. After selling everything I took from the house, I had $193,000. I plan to start my own business. Money does not buy happiness. Trust me on that!

### Victoria, age 28 from Ontario, Canada

I grew up in a Catholic church. I was taught that marriage really does mean "until death do us part." At the age of 18, I got married to Nathan who was age 20. We went to the same Catholic Parish and our parents were friends. It seemed like our marriage was arranged.

We were both virgins and took our vows seriously. Men are taught to be superior to women and are the head of the household. We have three children.

Shortly after the children were born, I decided to get a job. Nathan works at the church in the youth ministry. The pay isn't that great. Nathan was against me getting a job until I explained how we would lose our two-bedroom apartment if we didn't get more money.

I started working as a secretary in a nearby office. Nathan was very jealous and controlling. He called my job at least 10 times per hour. My boss told me if he called again that I would be fired. Naturally, I went home and told Nathan not to call me at work ever again. Well, that lasted a week. He began calling for no reason and I got fired.

He told me he was embarrassed that his wife had to work. He gave me a $30.00 a week allowance to buy groceries for the five of us – nothing else. As the kids would outgrow their clothes, he took them to the second hand store. I never got anything new. I wore the same clothes for seven years. He told me I could not talk to my own mother and I had to sit next to him in church and not befriend any of the other parishioners.

It got so bad that Nathan told the children not to ask me anything. He told them I was a child, just like them. Any questions needed to be directed to him only. He even stopped me from grocery shopping because I bought some Bazooka bubble gum for the children and it was not on the list. This is when I knew I had enough. However, I felt tremendous guilt because the Catholic Church frowns upon divorce.

I secretly got a job when Nathan went out of town for a youth convention. I took my children and moved in with my mother. When he got back, he was furious. He came to my mother's house and busted out a window. We had him arrested. I filed for divorce and it was final four months later.

# How To See The Truth

You are an adult and must make your own decisions. This is your life. If another person is making decisions for you and controlling you, this is a serious problem. Examples include:

- He tells you what you can do.
- He tells you what places you can go.
- He tells you what to wear.
- He controls all of your purchase decisions *(even for personal items)*.
- He controls all of the money, even if you work outside of the home.
- He tells you who you can talk to.
- He monitors your phone.

The truth is this has become a parent-child relationship. It is no longer a relationship or marriage between two adults. I'm sure you already have a father or father figure and don't need another one. You certainly don't want to date or marry a father figure.

# Regain Your Standards

Get out your mirror and take a good long look at the woman in the mirror. Now, tell yourself this statement. "I am intelligent and strong and can make my own decisions." Now starting today take your control back. If you are dating, now is a great time to end this controlling, parent-child relationship.

If you are married, you have to take steps to gain respect and independence. If you don't have a job outside of the home, get one, at least a part-time job. This is a huge boost to your self-esteem. You will feel important because you have somewhere to go and someone values your skills and talents.

Do you want to return to school to complete your college degree? If so, get registered even if it is an online course. Independence is the key to getting your standards back. Start controlling every aspect of your life. This way, you will be seen as an equal, not a child. Regain your standards and respect at the same time.

## Where Are Your Standards?

## Chapter Six

# DATING OR MARRYING A MAN WITH NO JOB

### Aahana, age 30 from Las Vegas, Nevada

I am a military veteran. I served a tour in Iraq. I am a college graduate and just purchased my first home. After traveling so much, I was ready to settle down. I met Reuben through a mutual friend. He was a great guy and said he was between jobs.

After six weeks, I allowed him to move in with me. He was going to help around the house until he found a job. He was going to cut the grass and do small maintenance jobs around the house, while supplying me with unlimited sex. A real "friend with benefits", right at my fingertips.

Well, this got old, fast. He didn't clean up, Reuben was lazy and inattentive. Finally, after six months I saw the light. He's not looking for a job, I am his job. He's living off me and he wasn't even good at keeping me happy. After doing some digging, I found out that he didn't have a job for the past three years. He had been living off women just like me. He also had another girlfriend and a baby with her.

I should have done some digging first before I moved him in. I felt used and foolish and finally kicked him out.

### Maria-Jose, age 48 from Santa Fe, New Mexico

I've done both of these. I dated and married men with no jobs. Cornelius was 15 years older than me. I was 28 and he was 43. I was divorced and had recently moved out of my parent's house for the second time. I moved him into my apartment after about a month. He said he was going to show me the world. Well, he didn't show me much of anything productive. He manipulated and used me. We lived together for five years.

It was so bad that my own mother wouldn't come over to visit with us. He took all of my money and my childhood collectibles. Even my prized possessions. When I became penniless again, I moved in with my uncle who took pity on me. I stayed with him for two years until I saved up enough money to get my own apartment.

This time, I married a man for all of the wrong reasons. I was 37 and Paul was 30. He was FINE, I mean Drop Dead Gorgeous. He was tall, dark and handsome, with a six pack, but that was it. He didn't have a job or a high school diploma. I have a diploma and worked at a law firm for many years.

Paul acted like he was my pimp. I made the money and he took it from me. As soon I cashed my check, it was gone. He spent money faster than I could earn it. It was spent frivolously on things like his hair and nails. In the meantime, I tried to come up with the rent money. Sometimes, I didn't even have enough money for lunch. I pretended that I was on a diet to save face. I hate to admit it, but I took care of a grown man for about 10 years. I think I did it because I wanted to control him.

He was my trophy husband. Everywhere we went, all of the women would drool over him. I knew he didn't have any money, so I thought they wouldn't be interested in him. Boy, was I wrong. He cheated on me all throughout our marriage. He used the only things he had, his body and MY money. I left him after he drained my bank account. You talk about a low moment. I couldn't even look at myself in the mirror.

# How To See The Truth

The cold hard truth is this man just wants to be kept. He entered into this relationship or marriage with no job so the standard or lack thereof, was set. He is not expected to contribute and has no financial responsibilities.

Since he has no job, it's pretty safe to say he has no place of his own. Most landlords or mortgage lenders are not interested in renting or approving loans for people with no proof of income. So he is living with you, or should I say living off you. You are now supporting a grown man.

The truth is he convinced you that you will have an ample supply of sex and affection. This is his contribution to the family budget. After all, that's all he's got to offer. In reality, you have your very own gigolo. A gigolo is a man living off of the earnings and gifts of a woman in exchange for sex and companionship.

# Regain Your Standards

This is another "get out your mirror" moment. Take another look at the woman in the mirror. You don't have to pay for sex and certainly don't need to buy a man. This is what you do when you allow a man to move in with you or you marry a man with no job.

Regain your standards today! If you are not married, put his things in a bag, call the police and have him move out. Change all of the locks, get a dog and a new alarm system. After all, this is your place and you are paying all of the bills anyway. Stop taking care of a grown man and make a commitment to yourself never to do it again.

If you married a man with no job, why did you enter into this marriage with no financial stability? If he lost his job after the wedding, has he been actively looking for work? If not, why not? Has he become comfortable since you are handling everything? Is there a reason why he cannot get or keep a job?

There is a reason why a woman takes a man's name when they unite in marriage. This is because the man is now responsible for the wife and children. If he has no job, how is he supposed to provide for his family? The truth is, he had no intentions of providing because this was not a standard for the marriage.

**If you have children, what are you teaching them?**

- Is it ok to use women?
- A man doesn't have to work to provide for his family?

This is the legacy you are putting in place. Children learn by example. Do you want your daughters to let men live off them? You did it, so why shouldn't they?

# Where Are Your Standards?

Chapter Seven

# DATING A MAN THAT WON'T COMMIT TO MARRIAGE

### Dana, age 25 from Salt Lake City, Utah

I call my boyfriend Kevin a "wounded warrior." According to him, he's had so many failed relationships that he will never marry. He also grew up in a violent family. His parents never married and never got along. I think this also has something to do with his decision to never marry.

After dating for six months, I found out I was pregnant. We had a beautiful baby boy who is now five years old. For five years, I begged and pleaded for him to marry me, even though I must admit that I didn't love him. I just wanted my family to be intact.

What I learned from my experience is that I should have listened when he said he would never marry. He has moved out and I am a single mother and a statistic. I was unmarried and pregnant. I am a high school P.E. teacher and teach health classes. I spent a lot of time teaching my students about practicing safe sex. Yet, I didn't. I feel like such a hypocrite.

### Addie, age 40 from Eugene, Oregon

I met Sean at church about 8 years ago. He played the piano and was a professional musician. He's been married twice before and told me he would never get married again. I am a widow with four kids. Well, being the superwoman that I am, I thought I could change him. After all, he was a church going man and I knew he probably didn't want to "live in sin", at least not for very long.

After three months, he moved in with my kids and I. He was a great father figure. My kids immediately started calling him dad. We went to church three times a week, twice on Sunday and Wednesday for Bible Study. We sat in the front row with all of the other married couples and I clapped for him while he played the piano for the choir. After two months, all of the ladies asked me if we had gotten married in secret. I always laughed it off.

Well, it has been two years. I gave him an ultimatum, marry me or move out. He moved out. I couldn't believe it. Then he began writing on social media how much he missed me. And like a fool, I let him back in. I found out that he cheated on me. I got up the nerve to kick him out again. I was so proud of myself, but it was short lived. I let him back in. We are still "living in sin" and attending church.

I feel so bad about myself. I have no self-esteem and I feel used and mistreated. Yet, he is still in my house and in my bed. He's not even a good provider.

He doesn't take care of me or his kids on a consistent basis. I know he's never going to marry me. I need help. I know I deserve better than this. I need to find my standards – fast!!

### Hannah, age 24 from Omaha, Nebraska

I was five years old when I met Gregory. He was 12 years old. His mother and my mother were best friends. We never dated and lost touch over the years.

Earlier this year, my mother called and told me that Gregory was selling some furniture he no longer needed. This was the same time I was moving into a new apartment. Naturally, I called him because I knew I would get a great deal. He came by my job to determine what time I would be available to take a look at the furniture. We met after work and I bought the furniture I liked and prepared for the birth of my son. I was four months pregnant and my son's father was no longer in my life.

Gregory and I hit it off. He moved in with me about three months later. He was there for the birth of my son and assumed the role of father-figure to him. We also talked about marriage and signed up for classes for couples who want to get married.

I go to church regularly and try to live my life right. Gregory wouldn't attend church. His excuse was the congregation was too big for him. However, he didn't make any effort to find another church that he was more comfortable attending. He slept in every Sunday while I went to church with my son.

We started pre-marital couple's classes. The classes were one day a week for an hour and a half for eight weeks. We only made it to the third session before Gregory backed out. I noticed some changes in his behavior. He was very mean and angry most of the time. He told me he was recovering from crack and heroin, but assured me he was clean. I never found any drug residue around the house. Believe me – I checked!

I begged Gregory to return to pre-marital class. He finally agreed. We had to start all over. So we started our second attempt and I knew for sure we would complete it and get married. The counselor said she never saw any love between us. I thought this was an interesting observation yet, I still wanted to get married.

Well, we flunked our second attempt at the pre-marital class. Gregory dropped out again right after our assignment involving the $5.00 date. This was the third out of eighth session, just like the first time. I got really depressed and started seeing a psychologist. He prescribed Prozac. That happened years ago and I'm still single.

### Chloe, age 28 from St. Louis, Missouri

Roger and I have been engaged for the past three years. We moved in together because we were saving for the wedding. He gave me a ring and I was so excited. There's only one catch. Roger refuses to set a wedding date or make any wedding plans. He missed so many appointments with our wedding planner that she dropped us. She had other clients who were serious about having a beautiful wedding.

We started a wedding savings account. However, I was the only one making deposits. Every time we got a bank statement, I found out that Roger was making large withdrawals. I was furious! He never explained where the money went.

My family told me that I am not engaged. Nobody is engaged for an indefinite period of time. They refuse to introduce Roger as my fiancé. He's referred to as my "live in boyfriend." My father stopped speaking to me and my mother refuses to visit. She doesn't approve of my living arrangements. She thought it was going to be temporary because we announced that we were engaged. Roger is still here and we are still not married. This really hurts and I feel so ashamed.

### Paige, age 33 from Spokane, Washington

I was a secretary in the Computer Programming Department at Sears, Roebuck and Company. Alfonso worked for IBM repairing our computers. We were just acquaintances and spoke to each other while passing in the hallway. I knew he was trying to make a move on me. He was very cute and I did want to get to know him. The bad thing is, I noticed he was going to lunch with a woman in another department. So, I kept my distance. There were two other men repairing our computers who were just as cute, so I knew I had choices.

Alfonso finally asked me out and we had a great time. He knew it was my birthday. We dated on and off for six years. We became intimate and all of a sudden no monthly menstruation. I am very regular and my menstrual cycle was like clockwork. I panicked and went to the doctor. I did not want a home pregnancy test. I wanted a professional opinion about my situation.

The nurse called me at work and told me it was positive. I nearly fainted while I walked back to my desk. I called Alfonso and said to him "What are we going to do?" This was when I found out that he is a momma's boy. He is 36 years old and still lives at home. I am 33 with a 10 year old son.

I waited and waited for him to tell his mother. That never happened. He said he was going to get me a ring when he got his tax refund. We picked out a beautiful marquee style diamond ring. He put $100 down and was going to pick it up in a few weeks. I was so excited!

When he got his tax refund, he didn't get my ring, he bought an $800.00 Rottweiler dog! When he told me I was not getting my ring because he spent it on a dog that was it for me. I kicked him to the curb. That was the most selfish thing he could have ever done. He was not thinking about me or the baby growing in my stomach.

He kept calling and I just didn't want to talk to him anymore. He stated he was still going to marry me, but remember he never told his mother. My sister took me to the hospital when it was time to deliver my son. She had to call him to come up there to meet his child. My son looks just like him from head to toe. He is a good father to him and still says he wants to marry me. Well, this has been going on for twenty years.

### Pamela age 30 from Reno, Nevada

I started dating Oliver off and on. I was at the age where I wanted to start a family and I was looking for a husband. Immediately HE was deciding our future. I thought I had found the one. He was an educated man with an advanced degree with morals and values. He appeared to be a man who wanted more out of life.

In the beginning, we did a lot of things together. We got very serious, very fast. He met my family and I met his. We came from similar backgrounds, but his family was more religious than mine.

We decided to become exclusive or so I thought. Unprotected sex is not my deal so for a while, we were at odds. I found out he was cheating on me. He claimed he stopped. At least, I thought he did, so I took him back. I told him I wanted a baby and if he didn't, we couldn't have unprotected sex. So he agreed and made this statement which I should have noticed was a red flag..."I will cross that bridge when I get to it!" Nevertheless, I proceeded with the relationship. Well damn, now I am pregnant and he decides to move to New York! What kind of man moves out of state when his girlfriend is pregnant? He can have all the women he wants now. Did I miss something?

I will tell you that I had already admitted to myself that I was going to be on my own. However, since I was pregnant, I told him we could try this long distance relationship. In my heart, I knew it wasn't going to work. I was quiet and conservative and was faithful to him. Oliver was just the opposite. We traveled back and forth from Las Vegas to New York. He wanted to prove he was being as faithful as I was. It was all unfounded and I caught him with his women and in lies and more lies. Too many to count!

All the pain and hurt didn't stop me from caring for myself

and my unborn baby. But it didn't take long for me to feel abandoned and depressed. That does happen to pregnant women, but I didn't think it would be me. I didn't have the support system that I needed. The struggle was real.

Oliver really never stopped cheating on me. When my daughter, Tiffany was about two years old, we visited him in New York and I found all of the evidence of his cheating and was done with him once and for all! Although I wanted a father for Tiffany and a husband for myself, the emotional pain was too much. I left him alone and never went back.

He tried to use a lot of reverse psychology on me and became very bitter. He had his friends badger me and try to give me guilt trips. None of this worked. After many years, I would only talk to him if it was about Tiffany.

As time passed, I began to heal from my emotional pain. He couldn't understand what I had been dealing with. He was STILL trying to control me. He would still argue with me, tell me who I could date, just offer any unwanted advice. All the while, he kept doing him. He also assumed I wanted and needed him.

When he came in town, he thought he would be spending the nights with me. He had the "baby momma syndrome." This just simply means a man thinks he can sleep with a woman simply because they have a child together. Well, he was sadly mistaken. I wouldn't even let him in my apartment! He couldn't understand what he did wrong. He acted like nothing ever happened.

When my daughter reached about eight years of age, I became very ill. I sent her to live with his mom. Now you know he tried to use this opportunity as a platform to prove that we needed to be together. Well, it was too late. He had hurt me too bad.

When Tiffany was nine, she came back home. I finally decided to have a talk with him. I explained all of my pain and hurt and why we could not be together. Wouldn't you know... he acted like he never done anything wrong. He even accused me of cheating and ruining our so called relationship! I said "Oh Hell No!" I kicked him to the curb for the final time and only texted him if it was about Tiffany.

I was told by many doctors that I was unable to have children. I asked the Lord to give me a child and if the man whom it was made with was not worthy of me, to remove him and I would raise my child to be a great human being. Well, he answered my prayers and as I stand today, I have a wonderful 16 year old daughter. It has not been without bumps in the road and the Lord reminded me of my blessing many times when I went left instead of right. This is what keeps me humble. I now know my worth since I have changed and I am teaching my daughter that she has choices and not to settle.

**Here are some important lessons I've learned as a woman.**

- What God has for me is for me
- No one will change unless they want to
- You are in control
- Don't doubt yourself
- Lift yourself up
- Be your own cheerleader
- Know your worth
- Stay ready so you don't need to get ready
- Cats always land on their feet
- You have choices

# How To See The Truth

The truth is, it is not you, it's him. You could be a perfect match for him. However, he is just not interested in getting married. Remember, you can't change him, fix him or cure him, understand this today.

If he tells you that he doesn't want to get married on the first date or two, be thankful for this. At least, you didn't waste many months or years before this subject came up. Please move on. Don't just continue to be friends with benefits when you know full well that this relationship will not end in matrimony. Cut your losses and continue to look for someone that wants the same things in life that you want.

Ladies, please listen carefully, don't get pregnant in an attempt to trick him into marriage. It won't work. A child will not make a relationship or marriage last!

# Regain Your Standards

You are still beautiful, smart and successful. You were just with someone (temporarily, I hope) that will never commit. I hope you haven't waited year after year for that romantic proposal, big, diamond ring and a wedding date set in stone. Remember my grandmother's advice "Never give your good years to a bad man." Take your beautiful, smart, successful self-right out the door.

Years from now you will bump into him. He will be old and alone because of his inability to commit to a woman. You will be walking hand in hand with your husband and a purse full of pictures of your beautiful children.

# Where Are Your Standards?

Chapter Eight

# DATING OR MARRYING A MAN WITH BABY MOMMAS

### Valerie, age 27 from Savannah, Georgia

I hate to use the word "man sharing", but this is exactly what I did. I had two babies with a man that already had two babies with a girl on my block, two with his live-in girlfriend and three by the girl that lived three blocks away. He probably has more, but that is all he would admit to.

I met Craig when I was 20 and he was 25 with seven children. I didn't finish high school. I got into smoking crack and dropped out of school in the 10th grade. He smoked crack right along with me. When I didn't have the money, well you know what I did and now I got two kids with him. I am now attending cosmetology school and trying to get my life in order.

He has disappeared and is not in any of the kids' lives. I heard he moved to Detroit, Michigan. Lucky for me, my uncle is a private detective. He is tracking him down for me so I can take him to court and make him pay child support. However, I don't know how much I will get since it will be divided among nine children.

### Violet, age 33 from Boulder, Colorado

I met Terrance age 35 at a club. He was the DJ and the center of attention. He was divorced with one son. He was a smooth talker and I was immediately drawn to him. He had a special spot for me at the DJ booth. I felt like I was the only one in the world and that he only had eyes for me.

Suddenly, he started disappearing and couldn't be accounted

55

for. I got suspicious and started to do some detective work. I went through his phone because he got a new one. What I discovered was shocking. Terrance had twin girls by a woman from Reno, Nevada. They were four years old. Then I dialed another frequently called number and it was a woman in Springfield, Illinois. She had a ten year old son with him. Samantha told me about two other children he had before she met him. They were 13 and 15 by two other women.

With all of these red flags, I should have broken it off. Why was I interested in a man with six children by five different women? I asked myself that question a thousand times. I never could find an answer. Instead of facing this question, I let Terrance sweet talk me and a month later, I found out that I was pregnant.

I told Terrance I expected him to be in the child's life. Eight months later, I gave birth to my son. Terrance still lives with me. He has a total of seven children with six different women.

I am an Accountant with my own home and I know better. Terrance tried to give me $75 a month for child support. This made me so angry that I kicked him out and I'm taking him to court for child support. Last week, I got a notice to have my child needed to appear for a DNA test. I couldn't believe it. Terrance is the whore, not me. He told me none of the other baby mommas asked him for money so why should I? I felt so foolish. I had gone 33 years without having a child, why did I settle for him? I guess I thought he would change.

# How to See The Truth

I totally understand that sometimes in our younger years, we make poor decisions. Sometimes, this results in an unplanned pregnancy while in high school or college. If this occurred once and he has grown up, learned from his mistake and has his life in order, that is one thing. What do I mean by having his life in order? He is back in school or has completed his education. He is working and supporting his child and is involved in the child's life, even if he is not with his/her mother.

The men I am speaking about have children by two or more women that they are not married to. Some of these men have two women pregnant at the same time! This behavior continues well into the twenties and thirties and beyond. Most of them are not supporting the children on a consistent basis.

The truth is women are nothing but sex objects to these men. They see how many women they can sleep with and don't even bother to use protection. If you come up pregnant, oh well, that is your problem. There will be no ring and no wedding. He'll move on to the next challenge. This is why television shows like "The Maury Show" are so popular. The women have to track down men and require them to take a DNA test.

# Regain Your Standards

Find out how many children this man has and if he's ever been married on the very first date. This is what you discover when you say "Tell me about yourself and your family." If he is evasive and seems to dance around this statement, he is hiding something.

If he has two or more children by different women out of wedlock, this means he is irresponsible. He could have used a condom. Why is he continuing to have children with women he's not married to? You don't have to figure it out. It's his problem, not yours.

Don't date men with multiple baby mommas. These men don't respect women and will not respect you either. He's interested in making babies, not making responsible decisions. They also come with a lot of baggage. You've all heard the term "Baby Momma Drama." Don't sign up for this.

## Where Are Your Standards?

Chapter Nine

# DATING A WOMANIZER/PLAYER

### *Kelsey, age 30, Miami, Florida*

I found a modern "Pretty Boy Floyd" and I wanted him badly. The problem was, so did everybody else in the greater Miami area. Clarence had the Miami Vice clothes and a following like a rock star.

We met at a restaurant. I was having lunch alone and he approached me. I am an Accountant and was crunching numbers for an important meeting. I was well dressed, polished in every way and so was he.

I asked him what he did for a living and he said he was a concert promoter. The "sensible" Kelsey would have bowed out gracefully. However, I was ready for some fun in the sun after relocating from Minneapolis, Minnesota.

We went out on a few dates and he said and did all of the right things. I thought to myself "Jackpot!" We dated exclusively, so I thought for almost two years. Then he became evasive and I became suspicious.

I got a hold of his cell phone one night while he was sleeping at my place. He had stars by each girl's name, mine included. I only got an eight out of 10?? I saw pictures of all kinds of naked women. They had taken selfies of their private parts and sent them to him.

I was so upset that I woke him up by throwing cold water on him. He told me to calm down because I was his "main" woman and I got all of the privileges of being with him. The others were just his sidepieces. I counted at least 10 different women in his

59

phone.  He said he had double that.

I felt so stupid, used and manipulated. I was on birth control, but he didn't wear a condom.  We had been dating for almost two years. I had started having some pain and inflammation in my private areas a few months prior. Yet, I still kept sleeping with him. Finally, I went to my gynecologist and she ran several tests and I got some horrific news. I have Gonorrhea, a sexually transmitted disease. I will never be able to have children. I am totally sterile and have chronic pelvic pain. I am so upset with myself for not protecting myself against this totally preventable disease.  I may have to have a hysterectomy in the near future.

### *Seiko, age 39 from Honolulu, Hawaii*

I've been sleeping with Malcolm for about 10 years. He's 36 years old. I knew he had several women and I hate to admit it, but I was okay with it. Even though we were living together, he rarely came home.  And when he did, I didn't ask any questions.

He had two children that were wild, undisciplined and just plain "bad" news. They came over to spend the weekends with us and tore up my apartment. Malcolm never chastised them and when I did, they would run to him. Needless to say, I hated their mother. She did nothing to help them become successful. They didn't do homework and got suspended from school at least three times each school year.

Malcolm got sloppy when he allowed the women to come by my apartment to pick him up for their rendezvous. That infuriated me! At least in the years past, he was discreet. After that, I kicked him out.  I met my current husband a few weeks later. We have been together eight years and married for five. My husband Jerry has no idea of my life with the womanizer. I'll be taking that to my grave.

## Bernice, age 35 from Anchorage, Alaska

I met Phillip at work. We worked at the utility company. Initially, I didn't like him. He just wasn't my type. He was a street dude. He was also a smooth talker and charming to the ladies. He had his own fan club of women.

Phillip was the typical bad boy. He was in a motorcycle club and a DJ at the most popular nightclub in town. When he worked, it was filled with at least 50 women.

One day, he was sitting in the break area talking to a few of our co-workers. I happened to hear the discussion about fishing. I had to join in because I've been fishing since I was 15 years old. He was very knowledgeable about fishing and knew about the different fishing reels and rods and what baits to use. I was intrigued so I let him take me fishing. Two weeks later, we were sleeping together and he was very good in bed. Now I can see why the women went crazy over him.

Phillip was living with his girlfriend Edna at the time. She was his main woman and the rest of us were sidepieces. I found out a few months later that he had slept with every unmarried woman at the club. When he didn't call or show up as scheduled, I knew he was with another woman.

I ended it eight months later after Edna stole his car and stripped it and tried to blame it on me. Why I didn't end it when I found out about all those other women, I will never know. Well, let me be honest, I do know. It was the great sex. If they gave out medals for sex, he would win the Gold!

# How To See The Truth

The truth is you are totally wasting your time. To him, you are nothing but a piece of meat, a notch on his bedpost and a booty call. All are very unflattering terms. However, this is how you've allowed him to treat you.

You know full well that he has several women. Yet, you continue to see him and spend time with him. What's most disturbing, you are continuing to have sex with him. Each time this happens, you're exposing yourself to all sorts of sexually transmitted diseases, HIV or AIDS. You're sleeping with him and everybody he's slept with. If this doesn't scare you, I don't know what will!

The truth is he's going to continue to lie to you and lead you on, just like he does all of the rest. You must teach people how to treat you starting today!

# Regain Your Standards

The only one that can end this relationship is you! You are not in a serious, exclusive relationship. This is not possible with a womanizer who has a different girl for every day of the week. He calls you at the last minute because someone else canceled on him. He often meets you after dark and doesn't spend much money on you just enough for a cheap hotel or he takes you back to his place. If he takes you to his place, he probably had sex with someone else just hours before you arrived. How does that make you feel? Remember, the words from Eleanor Roosevelt "No one can make you feel inferior without your consent."

If you manipulate this womanizer into marrying you, accept

the fact that he will never be faithful. He's always going to have "sidepieces" (notice I said plural). He is married in name only. Some of these men are so bold that they don't even try to hide their indiscretions. They parade their women right in front of their wives.

Leave this man and his parade of women alone. Get your dignity back while you are at it. You deserve better than this. The sooner you realize this, the better.

# Where Are Your Standards?

## Chapter Ten

# DATING OR MARRYING A MAN THAT IS IRRESPONSIBLE

### Octavia, age 23 from Idaho Falls, Idaho

I married William at age 19, both of our parents were opposed to it, but we were young and in love. We planned to attend the local junior college and work our way through college. William was an athlete and got on the football team. I was very excited for him. We both received our associate degrees and I enrolled in a four year university, William did not. I'm not sure why he lost his focus, but he did.

I was on a mission. I wanted to become a Registered Nurse and wasn't going to let anyone stop me. I begged William to go back to school. When it became obvious that he wouldn't, I told him it was time to get a full-time job. He got a job at Target in the stock room.

Our rent was cheap because we were living in an off campus apartment. I was still getting financial aid and this is when our troubles began. Instead of paying the rent, he used the money for new shoes and some rims for his old truck.

I got a job at a hospital so I could gain practical experience. I also started a secret bank account because I saw that he was financially irresponsible. I ate Ramen Noodles for almost a year because he never bought any groceries. He blew the money as soon as we got it. I put us on a family budget to try to get control of the situation. I started to pay the rent directly to the landlord myself. I gave him easy utility bills to pay, the electric bill, phone bill, and heating bill. Well, my phone has been shut off so many times, I can't keep count. They shut off the lights during finals week, all because he never paid the bills. I had to go to the library to study for my finals.

Because of my good planning, I had a substantial nest egg saved by the time I graduated with my Bachelor's Degree in Nursing. My family was so proud of me. At my graduation, I announced I was divorcing William, after four years of marriage. I moved to Atlanta and took a job as a nurse in a trauma center. He moved back home with his mother, flat broke!

### Tori, age 39 from Great Falls, Montana

My husband Brandon and I have two children, ages 12 and nine. We have been married 13 years. Brandon missed the memo "A man's word is his bond." Brandon is mentally irresponsible. He never keeps his word and it drives me crazy.

Brandon almost missed our wedding. His bachelor party didn't end until one hour before the wedding. His best man dragged him there and he was intoxicated. He told me he really doesn't remember our wedding. This is very hurtful. I told him to have his bachelor party a week in advance so he could have time to sober up like I did. My girlfriends and I partied for three days. Yet we were alert, well-rested and beautiful.

We bought our first home five years ago. This was not the house I wanted but Brandon didn't meet me at the open house and someone else beat us to it. I was so upset I was seeing stars.

Now that we are parents, his behavior still has not improved. I thought he would change after our daughter was born. Wrong! He missed the birth of our daughter. My mother took me to the hospital and stayed with me until I delivered.

He missed picking up my son from Karate so many times, it

became embarrassing. My son cried all the time and I complained, but he never made it on time. Some of the other mothers would take him home as a favor to me. Brandon always had some lame excuse and I was running around with our daughter and her activities. I thought we were supposed to share our parenting responsibilities.

The last thing Brandon did or didn't do I should say was deposit money in our bank account as instructed. I gave him the money and then waited a day before writing checks. Of course, all of my checks bounced. I was so embarrassed and was required to pay numerous overdraft fees. He said he "forgot" and went out with the boys instead.

After 13 years, I was tired of raising three kids. I kicked Brandon out. I feel like a huge weight has been lifted off of me. At least, I can keep track of my kids and my money!

# How To See The Truth

Irresponsible is an ugly word! It doesn't matter if the man is financially irresponsible or mentally irresponsible. Either one is a poor choice for you for many reasons. If he's financially irresponsible, that simply means he can't handle money. There are plenty of warning signs. Is he unable to budget his money? Does he have a place of his own? Is he paying all of his bills on time and without assistance? Is he financially supporting his children? Does he have a savings account?

If he's mentally irresponsible, that means his actions are careless and reckless. He doesn't think about the consequences of his actions. Examples include blowing off important appointments and meetings or he doesn't keep his word with you or your children. Everyone refers to him as a flake.

The truth is, the person is immature and not ready to be in a relationship or marriage. Simply put, he needs to grow up.

# Regain Your Standards

Age has nothing to do with maturity. You can't re-raise an adult. He's already had his childhood. Whether or not he's grown up is not your responsibility. Irresponsibility and immaturity go hand and hand. Neither one are desirable characteristics of being in a healthy relationship or marriage.

If you are dating, bow out gracefully. Let him grow up and don't wait for him to do it. Move on and continue dating and looking for your soul mate. However, don't make the same mistake again and date another irresponsible man, just with a different name.

If you are married, was he irresponsible when you married

him? My guess would be yes. If he is mentally irresponsible, don't leave him unsupervised with your children. Your first priority is protecting your children.

If he is financially irresponsible, get on a family budget and see if he will stick with it. Can he do it? If you don't see any improvement, remember you can't change him. What is your breaking point? Are you going to let him lead the family into financial ruin and lose everything you've worked so hard for?

# Where Are Your Standards?

## Chapter Eleven

# DATING OR MARRYING A MAN THAT IS EMOTIONALLY UNAVAILABLE

### *Cecelia, age 32 from Staten Island, New York*

I started meeting men on dating sites four years ago. It was very convenient and I've met a lot of interesting people. However, I must admit, I am ready to settle down. As a matter of fact, that was one of my New Year's Resolutions.

I called the dating site and asked them to change my profile to reflect that I was looking for a serious relationship. Before, I was more of a party girl. Then I met Walter. He picked me up in a beautiful limousine and we spent the night on the town. We really connected and I thought we would continue to see each other.

When the evening ended, I tried to give him my number. He said he didn't need it. If he wanted to contact me, he would call the dating service. When I asked for his number so I could call, he declined. This had never happened to me before. I am very sexy and I know how to turn heads. I've never had any trouble collecting numbers from men.

Being the determined person that I am, I decided to get his number and contact him anyway. At first, I checked social media and he didn't have a Facebook Page or anything else. I called the dating service and they had a strict policy about giving out phone numbers or any information from their database.

As luck would have it, I bumped into Walter and this time, I wasn't going to let him get away. I waltzed over to him and convinced him to give me his number. He was a top salesman for a computer firm.

We started dating, but I realized that he always seemed to be pre-occupied. He never seemed to be into me, even though everyone said we made such a cute couple. I had to initiate any dates between the two of us. He never called me. I always had to call him. He often stood me up, yet I kept calling. After about six months, I asked about his plans for us in the future. He looked at me as if I was speaking a foreign language. He let me know he had no plans for us. He was cold towards me. It felt like I was dating myself. He never had any input or opinions about anything.

At that moment, I saw the error of my ways. I was chasing a man that did not want to be chased. He was just too much of a gentleman to come out and tell me to leave him alone. I guess I was only thinking about my biological clock. I never called Walter again.

### Priscilla, age 40 from Wilmington, Delaware

I am a plus sized woman and I date a lot of men undercover. This is defined as a Back Door Girl (BDG). A BDG is defined as one of the following:

- A girl who enters through a rear-unnoticed entry to have sex.
- A girl you only have sex with and keep it a secret.

I've been a BDG since I was 26 years old.

These type of men only like plus sized women in private. They don't take us out or introduce us to family or friends. The men I've slept with have walked right past me in the hallway like they don't even know me. Many of us have self-esteem issues. We can't compete with the petite or medium sized women. They are the eye candy men gladly parade around with in public.

I have needs too. So I guess that's why I do it. It's just sex.

70

I'm not even a friend with benefits. I'm just benefits after dark in private. I know this relationship is going nowhere.

### Julie, age 19 from Bowling Green, Kentucky

I met Frank at church. He was 24 and very handsome. His grandmother and my mother were friends and we all attended the same church. We knew each other for about five years before he expressed any interest in me. He was a truck driver and made a decent living. I had one child from a previous relationship and he was great with my daughter. We got married after dating about nine months.

We relocated to Tallahassee, Florida. After a year of marriage, we had a son together. He was on the road five days a week. When he came home, he just hid in the other room. He never wanted to get involved with me or the children. It felt like I was a single parent most of the time. The following year, Frank got laid off. I begged him to find another job to support our family, but he refused. This went on month after month. His family was always interfering in our marriage. They were a bad influence on him.

We were struggling to make ends meet and I got fed up. Finally, I took my two children and moved back home to Bowling Green. I gave him an ultimatum. When he found a full-time job and a place for us, we would gladly return. I refused to come back and live with his family.

He was a follower and never made any decisions without his family. I told him it was time to grow up and be the head of our household. I waited for him for two years and he never came for us. He never called us and didn't come for birthdays or holidays. That's when I filed for divorce. It became apparent to me that he didn't care if I was around or not. He was married to his family, not me.

# How To See The Truth

The truth is, you are with a man who is not willing to open up about his true feelings. This can occur because:

- He's been burned by so many other women that he's not willing to take any more chances
- He doesn't respect women in the first place and simply wants to be friends with benefits
- He's not into you (I know you find this hard to believe). You are not the one he's looking for.

Either way, this relationship is going nowhere. He doesn't connect with you because he is emotionally unavailable and has chosen to be there. You can't change him, fix him or cure him.

# Regain Your Standards

You can't be in a relationship with yourself. A healthy relationship involves communication and if he's emotionally unavailable, he's not communicating. This is an easy one to remove yourself from if you are dating. He doesn't care one way or the other because he never checked into this relationship.

For the BDG's out there, you must get your self-respect back! Only date men that will respect you in public and in private. This is the only way to raise your standards.

If you are married, what kind of marriage do you really have? Was he emotionally unavailable when you got married? Did he marry you out of obligation? If not, have you had so many disagreements or "battles" that he's given up and refuses to check back into his marriage?

Sometimes, as ladies, we must learn to choose our battles. You can't expect to fight about every little thing and then expect him to engage in communication with you. You are quick to point out his flaws, but forget that you have them too. No one is perfect, including you! Don't run a good man away. Learn to talk to him, not about him and maybe you can salvage your marriage.

## Where Are Your Standards?

Chapter Twelve

# DATING OR MARRYING AN ABUSIVE MAN

### Barbara, age 33 from Providence, Rhode Island

Barbara read my first book "Center of Attention" available at Amazon.com and wanted to share her relationship experience and feedback after reading the book.

I am a survivor of domestic violence. A year and a half ago, I had to flee my abuser for my safety and the safety of my children after six years of mental, emotional, psychological, financial and physical abuse. My sons and I were exposed to extreme cruelty, mental torture, and physical abuse. My children were three and four when we left our abuser. It took courage to walk out and an education on domestic violence to get my life back.

I saw the signs that Debra talks about in her book before marriage, but did not recognize them. I thought my husband was controlling because he cared. It is only when I married him that I realized it was not out of love that he was possessive of me, but that his behavior was about power and control. I am safe and starting my life all over again and I wish every woman and young girl could read this phenomenal book.

I saw my entire life in the book. If our women were able to respect themselves, have standards, and recognize the signs of an abusive man early and walk away, we could save our women and young girls from domestic violence. There are too many women who are living in shelters in America because of domestic violence, it is an epidemic that knows no race, color or financial status. It has to be prevented.

Educating young women and girls on the signs of abuse, the

importance of self-dignity and having standards and confidence is the key. Women in abusive relationships need to know that they are not alone and that there is help out here and that they can lead a normal life and get their dignity back by walking away from abuse.

Please read this book. I give it an A+++++ and more. Debra is an amazing woman and her dedication to all women and young girls from all colors and races is amazing. She is a hero and a role model for all women for her dedication to the cause of preventing domestic violence and educating women on the signs and manifestations of abuse before they become victims of domestic violence.

I admire Debra Mitchell and consider her a role model for all women in America. I would recommend this book be put in every library in the country and every shelter and school in the country.

### Felecia, age 26 from Chattanooga, Tennessee

I had my first daughter at age 16. However, that relationship ended right after I gave birth. I got pregnant again at age 19 and again at age 21. My kids have different fathers.

Last year, I met what I thought was a wonderful man. Jose has two sons by two different women. We thought we were a perfect match, just like a modern "Brady Bunch." My daughters were ages 10, seven and five. His sons were ages nine and four. However, there was one major problem. He had an anger management problem. He blew up over the smallest things. I thought his good qualities would outweigh his bad qualities. I really thought I could change him. After two months, my children and I moved in with him. This was a small house he bought with his second baby momma. Six months later, we got married.

Shortly after the wedding, his abuse toward me and my girls became vicious and violent. First, he was verbally abusive. He called my daughters and I all kinds of names including stupid, lazy and sluts. It moved to physical abuse. He never corrected them if they did something wrong around the house. Instead, he just started slapping them around. They went to school with bruises. The school nurse called me and confronted me about the injuries to my five year old. I lied and said that she fell and got confused. She told me if she came to school with more bruises, I would be reported to the Child Welfare Agency.

I confronted Jose when he got home from work. I was sitting on the couch trying to reason with him. He threw scalding hot water on me. When I got to the emergency room, I lied and said I accidently burned myself. The nurse didn't believe me. She gave me her card and said when I'm ready to tell the truth to call her. She told me she's seen abuse before and most grown women don't accidently get third degree burns.

The following week, he threw me out of a moving car, pushed me down the stairs and broke my ankle. Five days later he twisted my arm and snapped my wrist. I was in an ankle cast and arm sling at the same time. I should have left then, but I didn't.

We bought a beautiful new home together. It had five bedrooms and a three car garage. Well, three weeks later, I had to call the police because he jumped on me again. He didn't like what I cooked for dinner, so he threw it on the floor and knocked me down with it and told me to eat it off the floor. I kicked him out and got a restraining order against him.

When we went to court, the judge informed me of all of his previous assault and battery charges, several other restraining orders and court ordered anger management classes. Obviously, he never attended any of those classes. I sat there in total shock.

I knew he had a short fuse, but I did not know that his anger problems started back in high school when he shoved his own mother. He is a coward who likes to attack women.

Our divorce is final. The home he bought with his second baby momma is now in foreclosure. I got the beautiful new home and he's back at home with his mother. I'm sure she'll be the next one to call the police on him.

### *Naomi, age 47 from Atlanta, Georgia*

I am a recovering addict. Crack cocaine and marijuana were my drugs of choice. In addition, I was a chain cigarette smoker. For 25 years, I was a functional addict until I lost my job. Within three months, I lost my apartment. For the first time in my life, I was homeless and went into a women's shelter.

This is a totally different world for me. I grew up in a middle class family and we all went to church every Sunday. I have a high school diploma and managed to keep several jobs.

Even though I was homeless, I was never helpless. I was divorced, twice with no children. My only focus was to get myself clean and sober and out of there. I kept a positive attitude and the counselor always complimented me on my ability to stick to the rules and move into a halfway house. They were very supportive. We were provided with bus passes, help filling out job applications and we had church services. There were many sermons on forgiveness and God's mercy. Boy, did I need to hear that!

After six weeks in the halfway house, I was clean and sober. Even though I was still smoking cigarettes, in my mind, I'd kicked two out of three demons. For five years, I stayed on the straight and narrow path.

At age 52, my mother died. Six months later, my grandmother died. I was so grief stricken that I lost my focus and started using drugs again. I lost my job because of my drug use. Since I couldn't pay my rent, I lost my apartment three months later. One afternoon, I came home and my stuff was sitting outside. The street thugs took my television, computer and all of my clothes. Everything I worked for so hard was gone. I only had the clothes on my back. At that moment, I remembered the Bible verse in the book of Matthew which refers to storing my treasures up in heaven where moths and vermin do not destroy and where thieves do not break in and steal. "You are homeless and using drugs again? "I delivered you from this hell once and this is how you thank me?"

I felt so ashamed of myself. I knew I had to get my stuff together. After crying my eyes out and apologizing to God for my bad choices, I started to see clearly. God put me in a shelter that didn't coddle us. We had to make it on our own.

This is when I went back to school and got two jobs. I worked at a cosmetic distribution center and at an airport. I promised God and myself that I would never be homeless again.

One thing the counselors told us was to leave the shelter alone, not with a fellow resident. This was our recovery journey and it was best to do it alone. Well, I didn't listen. When I saw Carl, he was tall, dark and handsome but he was also a crack and weed head.

When I was released to my apartment, I let Carl move in with me. BIG MISTAKE! He was always beating me and he was still using, even though I was clean and sober. I had so many black eyes, busted lips, and bruises all over my face and body that I lost count. The police were called several times and my injuries were photographed so I could have documentation of my beatings. The trauma nurse at the clinic saw me on a regular basis. However, I never pressed charges.

Then one day, he beat me so bad that I looked like I was in a car accident. After leaving the clinic, I went to visit my father. He was so upset and shocked that tears came to his eyes. He said, "That is not a man – He's a coward!" A few weeks later, we went to domestic violence court. This time, I pressed charges. He is in prison and I am finally free, Thank God!

Because of the abuse I had done to my body, I had to go on dialysis at age 64. A year later, I underwent a kidney transplant. My body responded well and I also quit smoking. I am finally free of all of my demons. I will NEVER date a violent man again. I have a new boyfriend who treats me like is queen. Life is sweet! I'm so proud to have achieved my status as a "Diva With Standards!"

### Michaela age 18 from San Antonio, Texas

I met Hector right after graduating from high school. I was still a virgin and looking for the right man for me. We dated for a couple of months and due to my lack of sexual experience, I became pregnant. Hector sweet talked me right out of my panties.

Hector was only 19 and he was not happy about my pregnancy. He didn't want me to keep the baby. He felt that I trapped him. Don't get me wrong, I didn't want to be pregnant. This was not in my plans either. We argued about him not using a condom so this was his responsibility too.

I decided to keep the baby anyway. That was when his behavior towards me started to change. He started slapping me around and pushing me. He called me all kind of names and since I was a virgin before I met him, I was really hurt. This went on for six months. My visions of us getting an apartment together vanished. I was too afraid to move in with him because I thought he might try to hurt me and my baby.

I cried for days and was very depressed. All of my friends were gone away to college and I was at home pregnant and alone. I never thought I would be a teenage mother. However, I knew I couldn't be around a violent man and I understood my first obligation was to protect my child.

### Sasha age 18 from Wilmington, Delaware

Robert and I were high school sweethearts. On the night of the prom, he proposed and I said "Yes!" I was extremely happy! As time went by, I saw how jealous he was of me. We got married in Las Vegas. We fought and argued the whole way there. I knew this was a red flag and almost backed out. I started to see how he was controlling me. Against my better judgment, I went through with it. I know what you're thinking. "This doesn't sound like a blushing bride who has married the love of her life." Well, I was thinking the same thing.

After we said our vows, we went to our honeymoon chalet and it was beautiful. This happy moment was immediately interrupted when Robert started crying for his mother. What? Are you kidding me? I didn't know what to think.

When we returned to Delaware, we bought a starter home and both of us had jobs. I thought this marriage might have a chance after all. One day out of the blue, he quit his job and left us struggling financially. He had an answer to the problem. "You get two jobs and I will watch the house." I said "Hell No!" After many jealous arguments, I filed for divorce. He came to me many times begging me not to go through with it. I had to. I was no longer in love with him and did not want him in my life. I could not be with someone who was that jealous and would not work.

To retaliate, Robert tore up our house, which was in my name. I had to get a court order to get him out of the house. He lied to my parents and got them upset with me. I love my parents and we've always had a close relationship.

Then things just got worse. He stalked me and I had him arrested for that! Even though I had a court order, he broke into my house. He came into my dining room with a knife and threatened to kill himself. He physically beat me like two men in a boxing ring.

During the divorce proceedings, he asked for things he was not entitled to just to drag things out. For example, he wanted my Barbie Doll Collection that I've had ever since I was a child. He also wanted my childhood toys. What?? Then he broke the tail lights on my car.

My marriage was short lived. We got married in September and I filed for divorce in November. My divorce was final the following June. It was a horrible experience and a lot to deal with for a 19-year-old.

### Monica, age 28 from Long Beach, California

In the beginning, I felt that everything was good. I met Otis while in college. He was nice, tall, dark and handsome and we had a great connection. That is until the honeymoon stage began to fade. He had his own place and I was living with my mom temporarily. You couldn't beat me going out south from the west side EVERY weekend. It felt so nice to get away and date someone who had their own! He treated me like a queen! He addressed me as a queen and every time it would just make me melt.

I began seeing signs with him when I would ask him to come

over to my place, although it was my mom's. It would be nice for him to come to me from time to time. He was very reluctant saying he wouldn't feel comfortable or just simply would not even come. I began to notice where it would be more of me moving around versus him, but I just let it go. I felt he was more of a home body and I was just a busy body.

Lately, when I would come over, he would imply that I am lazy because I was not working, although I was actively looking. He never paid much for our dates when we went out. I paid for myself because he complained about paying rent and child support and only had so much coming in. He had a three year old daughter and I was glad to see he was responsible enough to pay child support.

He had the nerve to tell me that since I had unemployment coming in at the time that I had extra money (yea right). He began to become short with me, upset when other men flirted with me. But I had no clue what he was talking about. Instead of breakfast in bed, he would be cold towards me and I would have to find something to eat if I was hungry. He was excited in the beginning to come home and see me, but then I would be left in his home alone for hours at a time. I knew then something was wrong but I didn't know what.

Suddenly, something changed dramatically for me. My mother was diagnosed with breast cancer and I was told she was going to have surgery just three days before our house went into foreclosure. It was only by the grace of God that my mother has now been a survivor for almost ten years!

But during that time, a lot of decisions had to be made, including where to move and all of the packing and stress that comes with moving into a new place. Naturally, I wanted and needed my "king" to support me. I began to realize more and more when I needed to talk or needed to vent, Otis would always change the subject. I began to pay attention and stop going to his home mainly because I was taking care of my mother and finalizing our moving plans.

The day was coming closer and closer to move into our new place and my patience grew thin. I began to notice that coming over to help pack and spend time with me was more of a task versus a duty to support his "queen" and her family in our time of need. I clearly remember the day when I asked him if he was coming over and he said yes, but he never showed. His reason for not showing up was because of his own memories and hang-ups. I left him alone because I could not believe how self-centered and egotistical he was! I wish I would have remembered that feeling before I went back......

Two years later, we came back together squashing whatever we had. I forgave him and we both moved on. At this time I had my own place, paying my own bills, working and having fun living life. He was between jobs and trying to make ends meet and emotions drew us back together. I upgraded my one bedroom to a two bedroom apartment and spoiled myself. Since he was my king, he was becoming spoiled too.

He still had his place but he was always over at my place. It was nicer, cleaner, more updated and I had cable a with a PlayStation 3 gaming system! Over time, he moved in. At first, he didn't like some of my friends because they were single and he felt they didn't respect our relationship.

We began to argue every time I would try to go out and eventually I just stayed home. On my 30th birthday, I had a big party and he became so jealous that in private he would push me in the back of my head. We were both intoxicated and he cried and apologized. On my next birthday, he was very rude and obnoxious to my guests. He became upset and demanded my complete attention on my day. I couldn't understand why this was an issue because I wasn't in his face constantly anyway, so why would I be on my birthday? After my guests left, words were exchanged and he got in my face. I pushed him in his head and he pushed me back so hard my feet left the floor and my head hit the wall as I slid down in the bath tub. The hair style I had cushioned me tremendously, but I still had quite a headache.

He cried and apologized again and again. He became more verbally abusive at that point. Also, he wouldn't talk to me or kiss me goodbye when I left for work. No sex, everything just began to stop little by little. We would engage at a family function and he would treat me like the queen I once was. And all I could think to myself was, who is this man? Once we would leave, he would not even speak to me. He began to control me. He told me where to sit, what to wear, who to go out with, etc.

The verbal abuse was exchanged for more physical abuse. He started pushing me in the chair and would hold my arms and sit on me to make shut up and listen to him. If I wanted to leave, I wouldn't tell him where I was going so he would grab my coat and we would tussle to the floor as I tried to escape his grasp. If I woke up and walked into the room where he was, he would roll his eyes and leave and go into the other room like I irritated him. When his best friend called, who was a single mother, she got all the attention, smiles and happiness from him that I once had.

I would lay in bed alone because, by this time, I got laid off and was depending on his income. Otis was the sole source of income. I remember thinking am I in an abusive relationship? I became so consumed with hurt and depression, and truly didn't know what was going on! When I spoke to him, he blamed me for hurting him and I asked how could I make it better?

Again and again, what I did was not good enough. I kept asking myself "What did I do that was so wrong?" I couldn't figure it out and he never gave me any clues. He kept treating me like crap over and over. I spent so long trying to figure out what was wrong and how to fix it, that I became more under his control. I wouldn't tell anyone what was going on with me. I couldn't go anywhere with anyone unless he knew them and they themselves were in a relationship. I ran to the one place I felt I could talk, cry, be myself and be safe. I ran to CHURCH!

I began to pray and fast and noticed that I had been so clouded, that I had been unaware of drastic changes. He was falling in love with his "best friend", the single mother. I began to find my strength in the Lord and one day I said to Otis "You love her" and the spirit in me revealed the truth. He snapped and began to choke me, pulled my hair, grabbing my hands and beating me while scraping my hands against a brick wall. The physical abuse continued after this revelation that he loved somebody else. I remember he slapped me so hard on the right side of my face, my left ear was ringing and my lip was split and swollen.

I remember each time he knew I was planning on leaving, he would somehow hit his head, cut his finger, twist his ankle because he played on my sympathy. I had a weakness for helping people. All of this was happening behind closed doors.

I fell right into working in the ministry at the church. I felt a pull to be in church, even though I hadn't joined yet. The pastor told me to "work with my wife for a while until you find your place" and gladly she welcomed me in and put me to work quickly. Every chance I got, I ran to the church, to the point my boyfriend got mad and left a message saying "what you keep running to church for"? You gonna make me come up there and clown." The stronger my spirit got, the stronger his anger until finally the two clashed.

Memorial Day weekend, we were at a barbeque gathering enjoying life. Everyone was cleaning and packing up so I tried to help him gather his music equipment. Whatever I said or the tone I said it in made him snap! He waited until everyone was in the house and he snatched me by my hair and threw me in the tool shed. He threw me on the ground. I was crying and yelling and trying to get to my friend's house. He was cursing me out and pushing me up the stairs and I was trying to get away. I was terrified.

A few minutes after it was over, his friend came by to give us a ride home. We were in the back seat. He kept whispering "wait till we get home" and I just looked out the window hoping the car ride would never end. Everything inside of me told me to go my mother's house for safety, but I didn't listen to my instincts.

I took my time getting out of the car and the driver sped off as if he could sense something was wrong. Of course, he dashed inside and I was still moving at a snail's pace. He came out cursing at me and demanded that I come inside. I was so afraid because there was a loaded gun in the house and we both know where it was. All I was thinking was if I go inside this house, one of us is going to die tonight.

Outside in the courtyard, he grabbed me trying to get me inside. He punched my chest, and all the food I had in my hands was thrown in the hallway and in the yard. He tried to take my purse and phone so I couldn't leave or call someone to help me. To add insult to injury, a young lady was seeing her man out the door. He saw my boyfriend holding me by my collar against the wall and he turned around and said to her "baby get back in the house and I will call you later." He never offered to help and she never called 911.

After becoming exhausted from wrestling and fighting, he was able to force me into the house. I was bloody, embarrassed and bruised and he grabbed me by my arm and sat on top of me. He looked me in the eye and said" You thought I would hurt you? I am not trying to hurt you. I will hurt me before I hurt you." This man is CRAZY!

Signals, alarms, smoke, fire and everything else sounded off in my spirit saying "get away NOW!" I called my family, I didn't tell them anything but "I need you guys" and in a flash, they were there.I moved out leaving basically everything behind. I regretted so often going back to him because my motto was "Never let your past come into the present because that will definitely be your future." Yet, I did the opposite. I had to learn that I loved so much, but love doesn't hurt. I had to learn and be reminded that God is love and God would do nothing or bring no one to harm you.

Since then, I have talked to him and admitted that I forgave him and asked God to forgive me for myself. It was not always bad, but the bad did outweigh the good. Now I know what to look for and what not to look for in a relationship and I thanked him immensely for showing me how strong I really am.

### Yolanda, age 32 from Bethesda, Maryland

I met Richard while working at a hardware store. We worked in the same department. He was age 27. All of the ladies liked him and thought he was very charming. We all went bowling after work several times and to other group outings.

He had a little girl from a previous relationship. I had two girls from my first marriage. We hit it off right away and started dating. He had a large family. Everyone welcomed me, even his extended family. I loved his mother. She treated me like I was her daughter.

Around our first anniversary, he asked me to marry him and gave me a ring. We moved from Bethesda, MD to Arlington, Virginia and lived in his family home. This was perfect for me. I had just started nursing school and was happy to be able to live rent free while in school.

Richard had an explosive temper. A few days later, we got into a disagreement and he pushed me on the bed. I knew this was a sign, but I ignored it. We went to get the marriage license, but I wouldn't set a date. I started to have second thoughts. He kept pressuring me to get married. I procrastinated and we got married on the last day the license was effective.

During this time, I was estranged from my family and was not in contact with my parents or sister. My parents relocated to San Antonio, Texas and my sister was busy raising her three kids in Salisbury, Maryland.

Richard was very bright and was mechanically inclined. He had a side hustle of repairing all kinds of things including computers, televisions, etc. He was good at providing for us. A few months after we were married, he lost his job. He told me he was terminated for attendance. I later found out he was caught stealing. He attended college and told me he graduated. However, he was never able to produce a copy of his degree. I thought that was strange, but I let it go.

While still newlyweds, we got into physical fights. There were a couple of times that I required medical attention and had to go to the emergency room. He even broke my finger one time.

Since I was a nursing student, I had to seek treatment at the same place I had done my clinical rotations. Fortunately, I didn't work in the emergency room and didn't know the staff. However, one of the nurses saw the signs of abuse and called me on it. I lied to protect my husband. I was so ashamed. I felt I had nowhere to go, so I returned to Richard.

He never jumped on me while my girls were with me. They spent every other weekend with their dad and the summers with my parents. I felt safe when they were around and tried to stay at work when they were gone.

Richard not only had a bad temper, but he also gambled. His whole family did. They would go to the horse races every week. They begged me to go along. To avoid another confrontation, I agreed to go, even though I don't gamble. However, I took my nursing books and sat in the bleachers at the top alone and did my homework and studied for my exams.

Things got a little better when we moved to a home that was bigger. We needed the space for us and the three girls. It was beautiful with hard wood floors. I thought we might have a chance and things would be different.

Boy, was I wrong. He smacked me in my face a couple of times. He kept pushing me and I pushed him back. We got so loud that one of our neighbors called the police. They took us both in for assault and battery. I got to return home, but they kept him for a couple of days. I refused to bail him out and thought he needed time to cool off.

Things were good for a couple of months. Then it would start up again. One night, I prepared dinner and he blew up because he didn't get enough rice. He threw me on the bed and then on the floor. I got so scared that I jumped out of the window on the first floor. He followed me and started beating me and then went back inside. I just sat there on the porch, stunned, upset and thinking about my exit plan. We had been married a little over two years and I knew this marriage was a mistake.

Unbeknownst to me, my neighbor Felicia witnessed the

whole thing. She came and talked to me and asked if there was anything she could do to help. I told her I was ok, but she knew I was lying. She became my protector and started watching out for me. My girls had become friends with her daughter and that gave me someplace to go if I needed to get away from Richard.

I stayed in school because I knew this was the only way to support myself and be able to get away permanently. Richard was so jealous of me. He resented the fact that I was still working and going to school and taking care of not only my daughters, but his daughter too.

The beatings continued and I started wearing long sleeves and turtle necks, no matter what the weather. One day while on rotation at a nursing home, I was requested to help bathe one of the residents. Another nursing student named Ronald worked with me. As we began to lift her, we both got wet and I had to take off my long sleeve shirt and white coat. Ronald saw all of the bruises up and down my arm and around my neck. He stopped in his tracks and said "Yolanda, what is going on and don't lie to me. Remember, we are in nursing school and I know what abuse looks like." I broke down and cried like a baby. I confessed everything. I felt like a huge weight was lifted off of me.

Both Ronald and Felecia talked to me all the time. They consoled me and told me "You got a decision to make. Only you can decide what to do." I began sleeping with a butcher knife under my bed. I knew it was going to be his life or mine.

By year three, I graduated from nursing school and got a job in Bethesda making more money. I planned to go into a shelter. Felecia knew someone who had a house for rent and said I could move there. Richard was not aware and I was so grateful. Now, all I had to do was figure out what day to leave.

While thinking about leaving, I suddenly had a change of

heart. I wanted to help Richard get his life back on track. I thought our marriage could be salvaged. I am a caring and giving person and he totally took advantage of me.

I had been saving money and wanted to help him get his record expunged. I hired an attorney and asked him to start his case.  He called me back and told me to "sit down". I did and couldn't believe what he told me. Richard never graduated from college. He got kicked out of college and served prison time. He wouldn't tell me what he did and how long he served. He just said it was "several years". I was so naïve. I thought he only had a petty theft charge, but I found out that I was married to an ex-con. His mother and no one in his family told me this.

Richard had a hard time keeping a job. I thought it was because of his bad temper - that was only part of it. The other part is that he failed his background check because of his criminal record.

Well, my window of opportunity opened two weeks later when Richard's car broke down. He managed to get another job in customer service and seemed to like it. He managed to work up to assistant manager. I offered to give him a ride to work since I was working nights at the hospital. He became angry again, over what I can't tell you, but he cursed me out all the way to his office. He called me every name under the sun. He had such a short fuse, that anything would set him off.  It was like walking around on egg shells every day.

Little, did he know, I was not listening to him, but planning on moving out. I told him that he would have to find a ride home because I would be taking the girls to a party at a hotel. I was one of the chaperones and would be spending the night with them. He was still calling me names as he exited the car. As soon as I dropped him off, I called and reserved a rental truck. I called my office and requested a week off. Then I called Ronald and Felecia, who had a husband and four sons. Everybody agreed to help me. I was so excited to be getting away.

I got to the house and we cleaned out all the things that belonged to me and my girls. Then I went to a women's shelter because I knew he would not be able to find me. I stayed there for a week. I was safe and began saving money for my divorce.

I had four months of peace. The house was beautiful and affordable. I was finally able to relax and I enjoyed my new job and my kids without Richard. Then suddenly, strange things started happening.

The house had a detached garage. Since I am a nurse, I work irregular hours. One evening when I returned home, I noticed the garage had been broken into. Immediately, I notified the landlord who happened to be a member of the police force. He had the damages repaired and started coming by to check on his place on a regular basis. I stopped using the garage because I was afraid to come in by myself after dark.

About a week later, I was leaving the hospital and arrived home at around 11:00 p.m. As soon as I put the car in park, I heard a hissing sound. All four of my tires had been slashed. It was only a miracle, that I didn't have a blow out on the expressway coming home.

The next morning, I was trying to figure out what to do. My neighbor came over and helped me. He helped me get new tires. When I tried to start the car, I heard a strange sound. I had to get the car towed. That's when the repairman told me someone had poured sugar in my tank and the engine was damaged. I was crushed. This was my first car that I paid for on my own. It was my baby!

I begged them to repair the car and they did. I knew Richard was behind the break-ins and the vandalism to my car. When I got to work, I went to the security department of the hospital and asked to look at the surveillance tapes of the parking lot. Richard was on tape walking around my car, but not seen vandalizing it. He was out of range of the camera. I was so frustrated; I didn't know what to do. Unfortunately, I knew I had to move again.

My mind was spinning because I didn't really have time to research a new school for my kids. It was in the middle of the school year and I knew it would be difficult to uproot them. I decided to take a couple days off to gather my thoughts.

The next morning, I was preparing to leave and opened my front door. To my shock, Richard was standing there with a 20 inch sharp knife. He pushed his way into my house and said "I'm going to kill myself and you are going to watch. Where is the bathroom?" My mind was racing and I knew it was time to save myself. My house had deadbolt locks that locked from the inside. There is a special way to unlock them that only I and the owner knew how to do.

I got my inner strength and kicked the knife out of his hand. When he reached for it, I ran out of the house and the doors locked behind me. Richard was locked inside and I ran down the street to my neighbors' house. We called 911 and they got him before he killed himself in my house. He was taken to jail and then to the psychiatric ward of the hospital where I work.

While he was being treated, I got a restraining order and moved in with my grandfather. The girls were spending the summer with my parents, so I was able to regroup. My grandfather was furious when he found out what I had been through. I stayed with him until my divorce was final and could move into an apartment suitable for me and my girls. This took me about six months,

Shortly after moving into my apartment, the rental office clerk told me a man came to look at an apartment and said he knew me. I was surprised because I relocated to Newark, New Jersey. When I asked what was his name and she said "Richard and he is dating my friends daughter." I told her that he was my ex-husband and he is very dangerous. I felt it was the least I could do to help spare another woman from the abuse that I went through. She said "He seems so charming" and I concluded by saying "That's what I thought until the truth came out." When I was getting my mail a few months later she told me Richard had remarried and was beating up on her too.

**Here's my message to women**

- Don't be afraid to speak up. Tell somebody.
- It's ok to be forgiving, but don't forget yourself.
- If someone loves you, they will put you in the front of their life, not on a back burner.
- Don't let a man manipulate you.
- Don't fall for their lies when their actions tell you a different story.

# How To See The Truth

The truth is abuse comes in several forms. Here are the main five types.

• Physical Abuse – is intended to cause feelings of intimidation, pain, injury and harm. It can also lead to permanent disability or death. Physical abuse can include striking, punching, slapping, kicking, whipping, beating, strangling, head butting, sleep deprivation, exposure to cold or heat, burning and biting.

• Sexual Abuse – is sexual activity without the consent of the victim, often with the threat of violence. If you are required to participate in unwanted, unsafe or degrading sexual activity. This is a form of sexual abuse. It can also include date rape and unwanted sexual contact between married couples. Men have been charged and convicted of raping their wives. No means no, even between married couples.

• Economic or Financial Abuse- occurs when the man is not supporting his family. The man is the head of the household and when he takes a wife, he has the responsibility for providing for her and the children. This is a form of domestic abuse in which the abuser uses money or lack thereof as a means of controlling his partner. They do not allow their partner to see bank records, bills or credit cards. Some refuse to work to make enough money to cover the household bills.

• Verbal Abuse - involves the use of language. It is a form of profanity and includes words that are insulting, disrespectful, rude, vulgar, critical and sarcastic. Often this abuser goes "verbally ballistic" without cause.

• Emotional or Psychological Abuse – is when a person lies, misleads or manipulates another person. It is designed to control and defeat another human being. It can come in the form of fear, humiliation, intimidation, guilt and coercion. It wears away at your self-confidence and self-worth.

The truth is any type of abuse is unacceptable in any relationship or marriage.

## Regain Your Standards

In order to regain your standards, you must understand the difference between victim vs. volunteer. If you witness abusive behavior for the first time, you are a victim. You had no idea he was going to act this way or display any type of abusive behavior. However, if you remain in the relationship or marriage, you are now volunteering to be treated this way. You've taught him that abusive behavior is acceptable. Remember, you can't change him, fix him or cure him!

Leaving this situation could save your life. If you have children, think of them and their future. It's much better for them to grow up in two separate loving homes, than one dysfunctional one. If your children have behavior or emotional problems, it could be related to the abusive environment they have been forced to grow up in. Give them a shot at a productive life where they can contribute to society. Otherwise, they may become juvenile delinquents or lifelong criminals.

## Where Are Your Standards?

Chapter Thirteen
# PLAYING HOUSE
## *"Living with a man you are not married to"*

### *Nicole, age 25 from Mobile, Alabama*

I met Jerome at church. We were at a Christian Poetry Reading event. He was a Christian Artist. A few days later, we connected on social media and became Facebook friends. A couple of weeks later we met again and he took me to my favorite seafood restaurant. We had a great connection.

We were both serious about our relationship with God. I told him I was living a celibate life. That's when we talked about waiting until after marriage to have sex. You see, I am a byproduct of an affair and I know how painful that is.

We dated about two months and suddenly my roommate announced that she was getting married and moved out. That put me in a vicarious financial situation. I couldn't afford the rent by myself. Jerome presented the opportunity to move in with him.

I am from Pittsburg and don't have any family here and only a few friends. I tried to get their approval, but I didn't. They knew the lifestyle I was trying to live and moving in with a man I was not married didn't fit the mold.

As I started packing, my landlord came to me and told me I could stay in the apartment. I would only be required to pay my half of the rent and he would give me time to find a new roommate. I knew that was my signal from God to stay in my apartment. Foolishly, I ignored it and moved in with Jerome.

I was supposed to stay in the second bedroom. Well, it didn't work out that way and we started sleeping together. I started cooking and cleaning for him. I knew he was the man for me. He was my husband. We talked about marriage. I had high expectations of him.

A few days later, I started to get physically sick because he had a dog and I am allergic to pet dander. I started taking allergy medicine, but it really didn't work. Since he saw how sick I was, I thought he would get rid of the dog. I should rank higher than the dog in my opinion.

This relationship brought out the worse in me. We went to two different churches. He wasn't the person he portrayed himself to be. I found out he wasn't even going to church when he said he was. I started to see things. As we talked, I could see we were not on the same spiritual level and we were not compatible.

After a few weeks, I became an emotional wreck. I started to feel jealous and insecure and started going through his phone. He had several female friends on Facebook and no boundaries when it came to the opposite sex. He never let me meet his friends, male or female and, what is more disturbing, he never gave me the title of his "Girlfriend or Lady." I had become a friend with benefits. After several requests, I got to meet his mom and two little sisters. His mom never opened up when I tried to ask questions about Jerome.

God was telling me to move out. He helped me find a new job with a higher salary. He revealed that Jerome wasn't a suitable husband. I didn't need to settle. I should have moved out then, but I didn't.

A few months later we got into a disagreement over some Oreo Cookies. It wasn't about the cookies at all. I felt broken, hurt and physically sick. I ended up hitting him and scratching his face. I was crying hysterically. When I calmed down, he forgave me. I constantly brought up marriage and his response was the same,

"We'll have to see." This is when God said to me "This relationship is a mess and we are not getting married."

Six months of this drama was enough for me. I sent a text to someone I knew that was looking for a roommate. She responded and we found an apartment and we got approved immediately. Jerome wouldn't even help me pack or move. He refused to visit me at my new place.

It was hard for me to focus on my new job. I prayed and cried all the time and asked God to heal my heart and send me a man that is a suitable husband. God answered my prayers. I stopped grieving after a day and a half. Currently, I am happily married to a wonderful God fearing man and we have a beautiful daughter.

### Elaine from 24 from Des Moines, Iowa

I was 23 when I met Tyler. He was 36 and also my boss. I had just moved to Des Moines, Iowa and didn't know anyone, so I just worked all the time. He was my boss for about nine months until he got fired. I never messed around or dated him while we worked together. I knew he had a live-in girlfriend at the time and a son. He was always flirtatious. He was touchy, feely, not just with me, but with all the girls in the office. It didn't come across as creepy because he was just a very attractive and charming person. All the girls wanted his attention. He got fired about nine months after I started for sexual harassment. Not towards me, but another female coworker. Upper management kept it hush-hush.

About a month after he was let go, he added me to Facebook. He sent me a few messages, mostly innocent. Such as "How are you? How are things?" Then it turned into "I'd love to take you out sometime." He stated his girlfriend had moved out and he was officially single. Of course, I had asked him about the circumstances of him being let go. He explained it was more of a misunderstanding, and that he didn't really do anything wrong. I bought it. This was in April, we went on two dates before he spent the night with me the first time. Not my typical way of doing things, but as I said he was very charming and could make anyone feel like the whole world revolved around them.

My lease was up in June, and low and behold, I wasn't renewing it. I was moving in with him. He had found a new job, but it was only a temp job at a bank. He failed to mention to me that it was only a temporary job and at the end of his contract he would be unemployed again. Also, to make this mix more fun, his elderly mother lived with him. He swore and swore that it was so he could take care of her and that she couldn't do the upkeep on her place anymore. But actually, she was paying most of the household bills for him. And when I moved in, guess who took over the other half? That would be me. I went from paying my $500 rent and $300 car payment to paying his $1500 mortgage and $700 truck payment along with my car payment and all of my other bills.

I have no reason why I did this except that "I loved him" and the "he loved me" and he asked me. He promised that when he was back to a better job, he would take care of me. I thought "ok" because I knew how much he made when he was my boss and it was six figures. We thought for sure he'd be making that soon again.

June was my 24th birthday. If I wasn't smart enough to see sexual harassment, no permanent job, and using his girlfriend and mother for money as red flags, I should have seen this event as one and it should have been my deal breaker. But it wasn't.

My birthday party was at a piano bar and my friends from

Iowa came along with my brother and his fiancé. It should have been a great night, but Tyler was apparently a belligerent drunk. He somehow made me cry. I don't remember why or what our argument even was about. But it ended with him and my brother in a physical fight and getting kicked out of the bar. Deal Breaker. Deal Breaker. Not ok with me whatsoever. My brother put my friends and I in his SUV and left Tyler there. He later got arrested and guess who bailed him out? That would be me. I guess my reasoning was I lived with him and all my stuff was at his house. Where else was I going to go?

Things only got worse after that. My brother refused to be around him, so family events were awkward. Tyler would get upset if I ever wanted to go without him. Also, turns out he had a daughter just show up out of nowhere. I had known about his son from working with him. He was really proud of Billy and was a really good father to him. He coached his baseball team and everything like that his daughter, not so much.

When all the court proceedings were over, she started coming for visits. He hardly paid any attention to her. She was three years old and she was adorable. I did everything with her from playing dress up and Barbies, to doing her hair and baking cookies. I was everything in that house. And when we broke up her mom called me to thank me for being there for her, and the visitations stopped shortly thereafter.

She wasn't the only "surprise kid" though. There were two more, with two different mothers. That's four kids, four baby momma's if you're counting. I learned about the other two because he let it slip when we were drinking one night. He had signed over rights to both of them, both boys. One was older than Billy and one was a year younger. Billy was 13. This broke my heart. I couldn't understand and still can't understand how

101

someone picks and chooses which kids' lives they are a part of, and which ones they are not. It was an issue he would get very angry about if I brought it up. So I just stopped.

This story only gets worse. On top of all that, he was an abusive cheater. So about five months into his contract, it was terminated. He had zero income. His mother and I were paying for EVERYTHING. There was NO extra money, which was a huge problem. Before moving in with him, I was in the mall every weekend and my life was fantastic. Instead of looking for jobs with all of his free time, he was flirting with other women. This happened either on Facebook, messaging them, or on free dating sites. I found this on his web history.

I don't know if any were over to the house or not while I was at work. He denied it when I asked, but I didn't believe it. He didn't even try to hide it from me. If I brought it up, it was my fault because I made him feel inferior because I held money things over his head. He claimed he just needed someone to talk to who made him feel better about himself. All BS. But of course, I stayed. My stuff was there and I was broke... where was I going to go? He reminded me of that too. He also made me feel guilty because I was just going to walk out on two kids that considered me their "stepmom." He was a master manipulator.

We had many, many arguments and screaming matches, almost on a daily basis. If it wasn't money, it was about some girl. He would of course just pick a guy friend or a co-worker to throw in my face, although I was doing nothing inappropriate. The first time a fight turned physical was when an online girl actually texted his phone. I'll be damned if someone is going to text him on a phone I'm paying for. He left it on the couch and I happened to see it.

I don't believe in snooping, he just left it there wide open. I

102

read it and confronted him when he came back in the room. Somehow that was also my fault for looking at his phone. Maybe I started that physical fight, but I threw the IPhone at the stone fireplace and it shattered everywhere. Now the real fight was on. He grabbed my arm hard enough to bruise it and had me pinned on the floor all the while we were screaming at each other. Once he let me up, I think I threw a glass in the kitchen and ended up with glass shards in my foot. I was going to leave that night. I grabbed my purse and went out the door. He pushed and shoved me in the yard and eventually I went back in the house. He got a new IPhone the next day. He said he needed it for the job leads he was following up on.

**There were so many arguments, all over the same things:**

- Other girls
- Money
- Him not having a job

He always flipped it back on me. If he was talking to other girls, I HAD to be flirting with other guys. He would have better luck finding a job if I were more supportive because obviously I wasn't supportive enough.

There were also a few more times things got physical. He choked me once during an argument and another time that stands out was when I was going to leave and he physically pulled me out of my car onto the ground with enough force to leave a bruise all down my left thigh. Then he had the nerve to ask me where it came from and was mad when I told him it was because of him.

For a few months, I was constantly covered in bruises. This obviously affected my job. I didn't want them to know things were

THIS bad. I wore long sleeves all the time, and I called in A LOT. I went from being a top performer to barely hitting goal. It was embarrassing. Not only did he destroy my self-esteem, he destroyed my professionalism and my reputation.

All this happened in a 10 month span. It was a 10 month relationship that absolutely wrecked my view of all relationships for a while. Not only did it wreck me emotionally, but also financially and mentally as well. He finally found a new job as a manager at a collections office. We got into a fight about the girls he was hiring. I knew he wasn't hiring them based on their qualifications and experience. He hired sexy, flirty women who would be eye candy in the office.

His first Monday at work, I called into my job and packed my things while he was at work. I was gone before he got back home. I stayed with my brother for two months before I was able to find a place of my own. Tyler had the nerve to ask to come to see my new place, like that would be okay. He thought we could work things out if we didn't live together. I blocked his number and blocked him from all forms of social media. It was the only way I could move on.

This was a huge lesson for me. Looking back there were SO MANY red flags that maybe I chose not to see then because I wanted it to work so badly. I just blindly believed whatever came out of his mouth. I think the important thing for myself and other women to take from this is, it's never your fault. As soon as someone tells you it's your fault and you made them mad, just run. He does not care about your feelings and will never be responsible for his actions.

Don't let them isolate you. This relationship made things very tense with my family, but in the end, they still loved me and helped me get back on my feet. Never think "I have nowhere to go" You ALWAYS have somewhere to go, even if it takes swallowing some pride and admitting they were right about the guy.

**So now I know better.  Here are the men to avoid.**
- No job
- Surprise children
- Heavy drinker
- Physically violent
- Previously accused of sexual harassment
- Not nice to his mother

You can't fix this mess. Even if he's not this messy, I won't date anyone with any of these characteristics anymore. I learned my lesson the hard way, but it's not one I'll forget. A man worth dating should add to your life, not complicate it. I should add, this was my last serious relationship and it was three years ago.  I've dated, but I have major trust issues now. So I don't just jump in as fast as I did with this one.

# How To See The Truth

The truth is statistics show that couples that live together before marriage have a higher divorce rate than couples that do not.

The truth is you are giving out an unlimited supply of milk and that leaves little motivation to buy the cow. You are also cooking his meals and washing his dirty underwear while helping pay the household bills. In his mind, "If it ain't broke, don't fix it". Translation, why get married when I have everything I want already? Why should a man marry you if he already has all of the privileges and benefits of a husband?

The truth is you've taught him that marriage is not necessary. If it was, you would not have moved in with him. Or what I dislike, even more, he moved in with you. In these situations, I'm sure you are financially supporting him.

# Regain Your Standards

Ladies, here are the million dollar questions for you. Why are you good enough to share your body, time, and resources with, but not good enough to share the same last name and build a future together? Health and dental benefits are not provided for girlfriends.

Do you already have children together? A mother is her child's first and best teacher. They mimic our actions, not our words. Do you want your daughters living with men they are not married to? Allowing them to use up their bodies, while they cook and clean for them? Do you want them to have children out of wedlock? You teach people how to treat you and your daughters.

# Where Are Your Standards?

## Chapter Fourteen

# DATING OR MARRYING A MAN WITH A SUBSTANCE ABUSE PROBLEM
## *Gambler, alcoholic, drug addiction*

### *Rekeida, age 24 from Cheyenne, Wyoming*

I met Benjamin after he sold me some steaks. He was the local "Meat Man" and sold steaks and beef. He started flirting with me and we finally went on a few dates. He lost his apartment about three months later, so I let him move in with my two children and I. This is when I discovered he was a drunk. He drank Jack Daniels, Cognac, Gin and Beer. He drank all day every day. He even drank while he was delivering meat. I could smell it on his breath.

Benjamin was never given a key to my apartment. I didn't trust him because he drank so much. He would be required to leave when I left and wait until I returned home so he could be let in.

About four months after he moved in, he came home early drunk, as usual and I wasn't home. So instead of going back to his car and sleeping it off, he decided to break into my neighbor's apartment. He stole his new 25-inch television. Then he broke into my apartment by breaking my sliding glass door and brought his television into my apartment. It was raining out that day so he made a muddy path right to my living room.

My neighbor got home around the same time that I did and traced the footprints to my back door. He saw his television in my apartment. I returned his property and begged him not to call the police. He agreed. Then I lied to my landlord and told him my kids were playing around and broke my back door. I gave Benjamin a good, old fashioned, beat down and threw him out. The following month, I moved to a new apartment.

### Rhonda, age 32 from Prescott, Arizona

I met Dexter at a convention. We both work for computer firms and our annual convention was in Miami, Florida. He was tall, dark, handsome, single, and had a professional level position. What more could a girl want?

Well, after dating a couple of months, John asked me to marry him. Neither one of us liked long distance relationships. It was very expensive and we missed each other when we were apart. He was living in Boston and I was in Prescott. I knew it was quick, but I agreed. We got married at a chapel in Las Vegas. Also, I am impulsive and make a lot of spur of the moment decisions. Most of the time I am right. This time, I was dead wrong.

Dexter moved in with me and life was good. We had so much fun together and we discussed starting a family. My mother told me to wait until our first anniversary before bringing children into the picture. She made me promise her because she said I really didn't know this man. I gave her my word. Thank God I listened!

About three months after our wedding, Dexter's secret was revealed. He had a serious drug habit. He did cocaine, heroin and oxycodone. He was able to hide it until he got terminated from his job. He wouldn't tell me why, but I suspect his employer found out that he was high at work. I kept paying the bills while he looked for work. He's a college graduate from a prestigious HBCU (Historically Black College and Universities) and I thought he would land a new job in no time. I watched him apply for jobs and I even helped him update his resume.

Four months later, I had to leave for a three day convention in Chicago. The convention ended a day early so I returned home. To my horror, Dexter was having a garage sale at my home. I had a brand new four bedroom home – fully furnished. The only thing Dexter brought when he came was the clothes on his back and his computer.

He had price tags on everything including my purses. I love designer bags and he had my Gucci bags with a price tag of $10.00, my Coach purses for $5.00 and my Michael Kors bags for $15.00. I was furious and called the police while I kicked everyone off of my property including Dexter!

He had not been looking for work, he had been doing drugs every chance he got. He sold all of my kitchen furniture, two of my flat screen televisions and my jewelry was gone. At least, I never opened a joint bank account and he didn't get his hands on my money.

My mother came over and we salvaged the rest of my things. We got a restraining order against him and I filed for divorce. I'm so glad I took her advice and didn't have any children with him. Now I can make a clean break.

# How To See The Truth

The truth is, this man is out of control and you are living with a ticking time bomb. I grew up around alcoholism and saw firsthand as a child the damage it does to the family. You never know when a person like this is going to explode again and the family is constantly walking around on eggshells.

The truth is, this person is often irresponsible, both financially and mentally. They are often abusive as well. All of these situations are deal breakers. All are unhealthy and below the standards of a healthy relationship or marriage.

# Regain Your Standards

Run, don't walk out of this volatile situation! It's not going to get any better until he decides to do something about it. Remember, you can't change him, fix him or cure him! You can give him all of the information on rehab centers or 12 step programs, but he has to make the call and agree to do what he needs to do. These are his demons and he has to deal with them.

You've heard the old phrase "You can lead a horse to water, but you can't make him drink." Get off of this roller coaster and take your sanity and your children with you.

# Where Are Your Standards?

Chapter Fifteen

# DATING OR MARRYING A MAN WITH A "COMPLICATED OCCUPATION"

## *Skylar, age 24 Philadelphia, Pennsylvania*

I met Kevin while I was delivering mail. I was a letter carrier and his mother lived on my route. I was familiar with his family because his brother was my best friend's husband.

When I met Kevin, I knew he was a drug dealer. At age 24, he had a new Mercedes-Benz 320 and bought me several expensive items a couple of weeks after we started dating. He bought me a fur coat, expensive clothes, and a new car. I must admit, I liked the expensive gifts and the attention he gave me. Within three months of dating, I discovered I was pregnant. Kevin bought me a house in the suburbs. I thought life would be good.

Because I am independent, I kept my job as a letter carrier. Shortly after we moved into our house, women started calling the house telling me they were sleeping with him. One announced she was pregnant. After doing some digging, I found out that Kevin already had three children. The first baby momma, Peggy had two girls and the second one, Amber had one son. By the time I delivered my daughter, Kevin had four children by three different women. Shortly after I confronted him about all of the hidden children and baby mommas, he bought us a bigger house with a swimming pool. He bought two more cars – a drop top mustang and another Mercedes.

I prayed to God to show me how to get away from him because I knew he was no good. He was selling drugs all around me now. I never did any drops for him. However, his mother and sister worked for him selling drugs all through the neighborhood.

God told me it was time to move and that's when I moved in with my grandmother while he was out on his drug run. I put all of the furniture in storage and was driving the Mercedes. When he got home, he was furious. He called the police and they showed up at my grandmother's house. They said the furniture belongs to the person that purchased it. I admitted that we were not married and I did not buy the furniture and agreed to return it.

Kevin begged and pleaded for me to move back in with him. I got weak and went back. Two years later, I discovered I was pregnant again. I knew I didn't want any more children – at least not by this man. Within a few weeks, I had an abortion.

You would think after all of this, I would leave him alone. Well, I didn't. I laid down with him and got pregnant for the third time. I felt so foolish! But, I decided to keep my child. I couldn't go through with another abortion.

I had gotten used to the women calling because I knew I couldn't stop it. One day I got pulled over by the police while driving the new Mercedes Benz he had just bought me. The police asked for my identification and told me they were seizing the car and all property purchased by Kevin. I was in shock and cried my eyes out. I was just a few blocks from my grandmother's house and she was there to comfort me. Then I called the new house and a police officer answered the phone. I asked if I could speak to Kevin. I could hear him in the background begging the officer to let me speak to him, if just for a few seconds. Finally, the officer agreed. He said to me "I'm going away for a while, but promise me you will wait for me." Like a fool, I agreed.

The police seized all of the houses, cars, jewelry, furs, wads of cash, cocaine, heroin, marijuana.. They took everything he owned. He was sentenced to 13 years and the judge said he would serve every single day. He would not get out early, even if he had good behavior. I was six months pregnant when he went to prison. His mother and sister had to appear in court several times. We all thought they were going to jail too. They took a plea deal and got probation and house arrest.

Then I made the biggest mistake of my life. I married Kevin while he was incarcerated. For the first three years, my two daughters and I went to see him every weekend, even though it was a three hour ride each way. Then we started going every other weekend. After five years, I stopped going and started having an affair. I was lonely and tired.

My life was looking up. I got a promotion at the post office and bought a house for my daughters. I was happy and had peace and joy in my life. Then I let the devil back in my life.

Kevin was released and we were now 41 years old. He was released around Thanksgiving. My family always came to my house for Thanksgiving and I was looking forward to having it with my husband for the first time.

My daughters and I went to the grocery store and returned with our supplies. I asked Kevin to get the groceries and he refused. He informed me that he didn't do anything like that. He slapped me around and cursed me out. He still had that drug dealer mentality where his servants or flunkies waited on him hand and foot. Well, that was not me.

My daughters and I checked into a hotel for two days. We came home just in time to prepare the meal because I didn't want to cancel my family tradition. My kids hated him. He had not been any kind of father to them.

I thought he was going to change. He did get his G.E.D. and a job as a dispatcher at a trucking company, but he was still selling drugs. He quit the job because he felt it was beneath him and was

114

too boring for the little money he made. He beat me up all of the time. We would fight all of the time because I discovered drug paraphernalia all through the house. He was useless around the house. I paid all of the bills and cleaned up behind him while raising our two daughters and working full time. After four months, Kevin went back to jail. While he was incarcerated for the second time, I got a divorce.

Kevin is out again and has a baby with a 25 year old. This is the same age as our oldest daughter. He now has six kids with four different women.

I found my voice and I am going to be respected! My daughters are doing great. God has delivered me from the devil for the final time!

### Abigail, age 18   Baltimore, Maryland

I grew up with a drug dealer stepfather and my childhood was traumatic. I never knew my biological father. My mother married my stepfather, Gary when I was a baby. At four years old, I was molested by an 18 year old family friend. At 12, my parents divorced and I was left with my grandmother.

Gary was nurturing when I was very young and I missed him after the divorce. Therefore, I begged my grandmother to let me live with him. After much begging, she finally gave in and I moved in with Gary.

At first, he would ask me about my homework, but that soon ended. He pulled out his notebook that was called, "The Cocaine Bible." He taught me how to cook the cocaine, how to measure it and finally how to sell it. There was a line of people coming to the door all hours of the day and night. They would knock on the door and slide their money and request through the keyhole. I would count it and determine how much cocaine they got. I did the same thing if they wanted hash or marijuana. Gary never wore underwear and I saw his private parts every day. The bathroom was filled with x rated magazines. I was molested from age 12 to 18.

It all ended when he mismanaged his money and went bankrupt. We had to move in with my grandmother. About a month later, she kicked him out because she found a naked woman in her bed high on cocaine.

### Cynthia, age 28 from Cleveland, Ohio

I met George when I was 21 while performing as an exotic dancer at a local gentlemen's club. I had only planned on dancing for a couple of years, just long enough to save up and buy a condo for my two children and I. My ex-boyfriend was killed in a drive by shooting.

A lot of drug dealers frequented this establishment. George, age 30 was a big drug dealer and had a lot of money and a lot of bling. He always asked for private dances in our exclusive room. After about a year, George asked me to help him plan private parties for him. He observed some of my regular clients which included judges, doctors, high school principals and executives. All of them were wealthy and I made thousands of dollars in just a few hours.

George was very territorial and discovered that a rival drug dealer was becoming a regular at the club. He didn't like the attention that I and the other girls were giving him. One night, during one of our private dances, he asked me to be his "main" lady. I knew he had several sidepieces, but I would get special treatment. We dated for about a year and I never wanted for

116

anything. He paid my rent and showered me with gifts.

Along with these perks, came control and dominance. One night after returning from the club, he gave me $5000 just for listening to a business proposal. Of course, I was all ears. He instructed me to arrange an after party with all of my regular customers and high tippers.

George gave me an address and told me to tell them to save their money and meet me and two other girls at a home for an "off the chain" private party. He promised me another $5000 just for getting them there and another $5000 for dancing for them. If I got two of my fellow dancers to come, they would get $5000 each. The party would only last for one hour. The possibility of making $15,000 in one night was unbelievable.

None of my fellow dancers would go. They warned me that I wouldn't have the protection like at the club. They begged me not to go. They all knew George and his reputation. I just felt they didn't know him since he was my man.

I decided to go and keep all the money for myself. I guess you can say I was greedy. Right after I arrived, I began dancing and the tips started flowing. George offered all of the men drinks and drugs, including cocaine and heroin. About a half hour into my routine, all hell broke out. George decided to rob them all. He pulled out a gun and shot it in the air. He ordered everyone to give up their money, jewelry, keys and cell phones. I sat there in shock. When I wasn't moving, he pointed the gun at me and ordered me to collect all of their stuff. I did what I was told and put all of the items in a large bag he gave me.

I started crying and begged him to let me go. Two of the men fought back and one got shot in the stomach. During the commotion, I ran out the front door with nothing but a string bikini on. George threw three stacks of money at me and told me to forget everything that I saw, each contained $5000. I grabbed my money and left. The next day, I called the club and quit. This was my sign to get out of this lifestyle. I also broke up with George. This was too much for me. I had never been so scared in my entire life.

About a month later, a detective banged on my door. It was so loud that it frightened my kids, ages two and four. I opened the door and they started questioning me about the night of the robbery and shooting. I was taken into custody. My mother had to come to the police station to get my kids.

I told them the truth and that I didn't know anyone was going to get hurt. I was there to dance and collect money for entertaining them. He asked me if I helped plan the party. I admitted that I did at George's request. Both of us were charged with robbery and attempted murder. George was also charged with drug trafficking. I was in shock!!

After many months, I took a plea deal and was sentenced to six years. My mother went to court and got custody of my kids. They are now eight and 10 and won't speak to me, neither will my mother.

I'm going to parenting classes and trying to regain custody of my children. I miss them so much. My mother told me the whole family has disowned me. She said she is going to fight me to retain custody. She doesn't think I am a good influence on my own kids. I'm currently living in a rundown apartment complex and working in a bowling alley.

# How To See The Truth

The truth is he is involved in illegal activities and he is going to get caught sooner or later. Everything he has obtained is going to get seized by the police and he will do jail time. You will probably be going right along with him if you don't get out. These situations turn very ugly, very fast!

# Regain Your Standards

There is no easy way to say this, so I'm just going to say it. Illegal activities lead to jail or death. You don't want all kind of criminals coming to your home or around your children. If you don't get out today, you could lose everything including your freedom and your life. Your children are in harm's way!

Today, Now, This Second, Get out and Stay Out! Then make a vow never to date or marry this type of man again.

# Where Are Your Standards?

## Chapter Sixteen

# DATING OR MARRYING A MAN WITH EX-WIVES

## *Tanisha, age 40 from Tulsa, Oklahoma*

I met Blair, age 39 at a grand opening. He was a popular news reporter. He was very polished and professional. After a little small talk, he asked me out. During our first date, I asked him to tell me about himself. This is when I discovered he was recently divorced, for the third time. I knew this was cause for concern, so I decided to take good mental notes. I have never been married and have no children.

About two months later, I introduced him to my mother. He tried to win her over with his lucrative salary, but when she asked about his past marriages, she was not impressed. She told me the old phrase "Everything that glitters is not gold." Naturally, I defended him and blamed all of the failed marriages on the ex-wives. He's a good man and a good father who loves his 10 year old son.

At his family picnic over the summer, I got a lot of strange looks and couldn't figure out why. Then his father said to me "You won't be around long." I was confused and asked him what he meant by that. He refused to answer and walked away. I confronted Blair about his fathers' strange comment. He just said his family was crazy and that's why he didn't want to come in the first place.

We dated nine months then he asked me to marry him. Since I'd never been married, I accepted. The pickings get a little slim for women in their 40's. He moved into my house because he said his three former wives cleaned him out and his check was garnished for child support. I'm a school administrator and I welcomed my new husband into my home. Two months after we returned from our honeymoon in the Bahamas, the truth came out.

Even though he made a good salary, he had nothing to show for it. Even after the deduction for child support, he still should have had some disposable income to contribute to our family household expenses. We calculated what he was supposed to contribute each month and opened up a joint bank account. My check was direct deposited from my employer. I assumed his was too.

When the bank statements arrived, the account was nearly empty. When I confronted Blair, he said it was a problem with his payroll department and he was going to straighten it out. This went on for another couple of months until I decided to hire a private detective and put a GPS on his car. I thought he was having an affair. I was wrong. He had a chronic gambling problem! Blair was at several casinos spending four to six hours there each day. I sat there in disbelief.

A couple of days later, I picked his son up from the child's mother, Veronica as a favor to him. We got along just fine. We struck up a conversation and she told me that she didn't take him to the cleaners; he gambled away everything except the shirt on his back. He even stole the money from his own son who was saving to buy new video games.

His gambling was the reason she and the other two wives divorced him. Veronica told me he was not allowed in his parent's home because he's stolen from them so many times, he's no longer welcome. I thought it was strange that we didn't visit. But after my experience at the picnic, I thought his family was just weird.  She advised me to get a different bank account ASAP! I left her home and went straight to the bank. Blair cleaned it out – Again!

My private detective had more evidence of him at casinos when he was supposed to be covering a story. His station manager put him on probation. On my first anniversary, I was in my attorney's office filing for divorce. Now I understand what his father meant at the picnic.

### Edna age 32 from Jackson, Mississippi

I met Melvin at a wedding reception.  I caught the bouquet and all of the men knew I was single. We danced a couple of times and he asked me for my number. Melvin was 37 years old and a Certified Public Accountant (CPA). He had one daughter age 17. I was an Administrative Assistant at a high school. He was a smooth talker and very good looking. I was immediately drawn to him and vice versa.

What I liked most about him was the unusual places he would pick for our dates. Everybody goes out to dinner. Melvin would pick places like the museums, jazz concerts, picnics in the park and weekend getaways. He also kept his condo in immaculate condition.

After three months, I started really getting to know him.  He was a good man with a good heart. One night at the candlelight bowling, he told me about his past. He was divorced, not once, not twice, but three times. I sat there in shock because I had never met anyone who had been married so many times. He reminded me of the actors in Hollywood with multiple ex-wives.

I asked him why his marriages failed. He admitted he was never faithful. He swore that he had learned from his mistakes and was finished sowing his "wild oats" years ago. He had been divorced for five years and was looking for the right women and to do things right this time.

We continued seeing each other and started to fall in love. We dated for a year and I thought we were exclusive. That is until his cell phone started blowing up. Suddenly, he was late for our dates or would cancel them altogether. He claimed he had some business deals and it was tax season. He saw how upset I was and surprised me with a trip to Hawaii where he proposed.

We were so excited and three months later, we were married. We had a beautiful ceremony with all of our friends and family in Jackson. Two years went by without a hitch. We wanted to start a family and the following year our daughter Melissa was born.

I was fortunate enough to become a stay at home mom. That is when the truth came out. Melvin had several "sidepieces" all throughout our marriage! It was time to nail him to the wall.

One night, I asked him to give Melissa a bath. I knew this would take him a while so I could do my detective work. I knew the code to his phone because I was with him when he upgraded it. I went through the photos and saw pictures of women with their private parts exposed. So what did I do? I called the very first one. Her name was Bernice. She said she didn't know Melvin was married and only knew of his 17 year old daughter.

She met our two year old daughter at his mother's birthday party in Biloxi when he introduced her as his niece! What kind of man is he? This was his flesh and blood. The reason I didn't attend was because I had broken my ankle when I was jogging a few days before her party. I sent my husband and daughter and my mother-in-law assured me she would watch Melissa. This tramp told me that Melvin left Melissa with his mother and spent the weekend with her.  I was furious but knew I had to keep my cool.

I called my brother and told him to meet me at the U-Haul in the morning at 9:00 a.m. Then I returned to the kitchen and made dinner as if nothing happened.  I was tempted to put some poison in his food, but decided against that. I ain't going to jail for no low down dog! All night my head was spinning. I couldn't wait until morning.

Melvin left for the office at 8:30 a.m. as usual. At 9:00 a.m. my brother met me at the U-Haul with two of his friends. We cleaned out the entire condo with the exception of the bed. You see, I moved into his condo after our wedding and he probably had all kind of tramps in there. We were done at about 1:00 p.m. I moved into my brother's rental property that was in a gated community on the 3rd floor.  I felt perfectly safe.  Also, I got a dog.

**I wrote the following poem and left it on his pillow.**

*I guess you think I am a fool,*
*And you can hide your multiple rendezvous'.*
*Now I see why you've been married multiple times,*
*You still chasing any skirt you can find.*
*According to your tramp Bernice,*
*Our daughter Melissa is your niece!*
*I bet it's clear, I want a divorce,*
*And you WILL pay alimony and child support!!*

# How To See The Truth

If he is a widower, that is a different story. He lived out his vows until his wife passed away and they were separated by death. However, if he has a string of failed marriages, this has occurred for a reason. It is him or his habits. He's the common denominator.

I'm sure he blamed the first marriage on immaturity and bad judgment. However, if you are looking at a man who has been married 2,3,4,5 times, this is a red flag!

The truth is statistics show that people with multiple marriages have higher divorce rates than other groups. Why does he have so many bad marriages? You may never know. I'm sure he blames all of the problems on his ex-wife. We both know it takes two to tango and there are two sides to every story. However, the odds are already stacked against this relationship lasting a lifetime.

# Regain Your Standards

You will be able to determine why he's had so many failed marriages if you do a little homework. Is he abusive in any way? Does he have an anger management problem? Is he addicted to a substance? Is he irresponsible? All of these are red flags. If you are dating, this relationship is not worthy of putting any more time or energy into it. Why wait around and become wife number five just to become divorced a short time later?

If you are married, I'm sure it's safe to say you didn't do your homework or chose to ignore all of the red flags that were right in your face. You already know you can't change him, fix him or cure him. Now you see the signs and must decide what to do. You have options.

# Where Are Your Standards?

## Chapter Seventeen

# MARRYING A MAN YOU BARELY KNOW

### *June, age 20 from Portland, Maine*

I met Demetrius through a mutual friend. He was 35 years old. I was surprised that someone that old would be interested in me. He seemed so mature. We dated three months and he asked me to marry him. I said yes for one reason, I wanted to move out of my parent's house. I was sharing a room with my sister and we had bunk beds. It felt cramped with no privacy and I knew it was time to go. Demetrius was my ticket out.

In my heart, I knew this was a big mistake. I was not in love with him. As a matter of fact, I spent the night with my ex-boyfriend the night before and was almost late for the wedding. Luckily for me, it was in my parents' living room. Demetrius was no catch. My father had to lend him a suit for the wedding ceremony, another bad sign!

My marriage went south very fast. He was a violent man who drank too much. He was very confrontational and started arguments over small things. Instead of working through problems, he started drinking and beating me.

One night, my neighbor knocked on my door and told me my husband was passed out in the staircase. I was a big, strong girl and was able to drag him back into the apartment. Looking back, I should have left him out there.

Our eight month marriage ended in divorce the night he stabbed me in my chest. I still have the stab wound which is right between my breasts. I can't wear v-shaped blouses because I need to cover up the scar so I don't have to think about him when

I look in the mirror.

### *Brittany age 19 Sioux Falls, South Dakota*

I married Arnold before I got to know him. We got married four months after meeting at a church function. I was a single mother and looking for a father for my daughter. My ex-boyfriend left me while I was pregnant. He said he wasn't the father and won't have anything to do with us. I am still trying to get him to submit to a DNA test so he can start paying child support.

Arnold was a nice man and I tried to make myself fall in love with him. We even had a daughter together. He was a good father, but not a good husband. We fought because we had nothing in common. I am an extrovert and he was an introvert. He never wanted to go anyplace or do anything with me. I knew I didn't love him and filed for divorce. We were married three years.

Looking back, I had no business marrying him. I wanted a father figure and that is what drove me into this marriage. I never loved him and I am ashamed of myself for tricking him.

# How To See The Truth

The truth is this is the number one common mistake of all of the women I interviewed. As you can see, they were running from a bad situation instead of running into a loving marriage. Marrying a man you've only known for a few months often ends in divorce.

Many young women are ready to leave home but don't know how to do it. They lack self-confidence and have never been taught the skills to be self-sufficient in the world. So instead of preparing themselves for independence, they latch on the first man they can. It doesn't matter if he is a suitable companion or not.

The truth is, you thought this man was your winning ticket out of the house and into the world where "they lived happily ever after." Instead of getting the grand prize, you got the booby prize and found yourself in a bed with a man who is just like a stranger to you.

# Regain Your Standards

It's time to grow up and do your homework. You know the signs of abuse and what to look for. There are a lot of great guys out there. Do you have one or not? Do your homework and determine if you love him or not. If you do, work with him to build a life together. Work is an action word and be prepared to work hard for your marriage.

Life is short. If you determine you don't love him, let him go so he can find someone who does. Don't lie to yourself and don't live in denial. You can't find your soul mate if you are tied to him.

# Where Are Your Standards?

## Chapter Eighteen

# MARRYING A MAN JUST BECAUSE YOU ARE PREGNANT OR ALREADY HAVE A CHILD TOGETHER

### *Lana, age 27 from Boston, Massachusetts*

I moved in with my boyfriend with one thing in mind, to get pregnant and to get married. I have to admit the truth, I didn't want to work. I graduated from high school early and completed one semester of college, but hated it and didn't do very well. Since I am good in sales, I got a job selling cell phones. However, I didn't see this as a long-term career. I am very attractive and have lived with three different men. All of the relationships ended badly because I cheated on them and they caught me.

David had a college degree. We met at a college party. I lied to him and told him I was in school. When the semester ended, I relocated and got another job selling beer and wines. We reconnected about three years later and he asked me to move in with him. I gladly moved from Boston to Las Vegas.

David had a one bedroom apartment and worked at a beverage company and was the assistant coach at a local high school. We lived together four months when I discovered I was pregnant. I knew I wasn't taking any birth control. David was surprised, but came from a nice family so we got married when I was five months pregnant. We really couldn't afford a honeymoon and when the baby was born, we moved in with his family.

His family consisted of his mother, father, two sisters,

brother, and grandmother. We lived in a three bedroom home and it was very crowded. We had no privacy and sex was non-existent. I was so unhappy. I rushed into this thinking that I would be living like a princess.

After one year his father has asked us to leave. David told me it was time for me to find a job. I worked as a nanny watching two children while their mom worked, but it was not enough. David was very mean to me and my son. I heard him tell his dad that I ruined his life. He was doing just fine before I came around.

David bought me a one-way ticket to Boston. He told me to get out and don't return. He was filing for divorce. I begged him to reconsider, but it was too late. I really thought we could grow to love each other. With no other choice, I packed my bags and moved in with my grandmother. Two days later, the divorce papers were served. I thought our son would keep us together. What I have learned is that you can't use a child to trap a man.

### Tammy, age 25 from Burlington, Vermont

I met Clint, age 26 at a party. We were both college students. Clint finished college, but I dropped out. I am a product of an affair and Clint's parents never married. Somehow, that was what we felt we had in common.

After six months of dating, we moved into an apartment together. I was working at the post office and he had an office job. We planned to have a child together and I got pregnant. I know full well that a 25-year-old doesn't "accidently" come up pregnant. We both knew what we were doing.

After having my son, I moved back home. I just wanted to be around my family with my newborn. Even though I had no intentions of having another child out of wedlock, I found out I was pregnant for the second time. I grew up in the church, I knew better. I did not want to be like my mother. Yet, I found myself unmarried and pregnant just like her.

I begged Clint to marry me before the birth of our second child. We got married when I was four months pregnant. We had three more children together within the next five years.

After having all of the children and moving into our home, I thought we would live happily ever after. What I discovered is that we are not compatible. We just don't get along. We don't love each other. I was trying to save face instead of facing my insecurities. I felt pressured to get married and start a family just like everybody I grew up with.

But just like most of them, I am divorced.

# How To See The Truth

The truth is this has been going on for centuries. It is called a shotgun wedding. That means a wedding that is arranged to avoid embarrassment due to an unplanned pregnancy. It can be traced back to the 18th century.

The truth is most shotgun weddings end in divorce. The only thing you have in common is a baby. This just means you had unprotected sex. It doesn't mean you love each other and are committed to each other. So why stay together? The child deserves to grow up in a loving environment.

The truth is if you were not pregnant, would you have married him? I already know the answer. It is no.

# Regain Your Standards

You deserve to be happy and so does the child. Why compound one mistake, and unplanned pregnancy with another, marrying a man you do not love?

Regain your standards today. Plan to co-parent with the father of your child. Make a commitment to yourself to not have unprotected sex until you marry the man of your dreams. I recommend you wait a year before having any more children. This way, you can give the marriage a chance before adding more responsibilities. The child you bring with you must be loved by his parents and step parents.

Time to grow up! You don't need to trap a man into marriage. You can't make him love you or stay with you for a lifetime.

# Where Are Your Standards?

# Chapter Nineteen

# DATING OR MARRYING A MAN THAT DOESN'T SUPPORT HIS CHILDREN

### *Josephina, age 36 from Charleston, West Virginia*

I met Ian at a sporting event. He was a hustler. He had never been married but had two children by two different women. His oldest son was a teenager and he only saw him once or twice a year. His daughter was six years old and the mother wouldn't allow him to see her because he refused to pay child support.

Ian likes to play pool and enters pool tournaments. He banks on winning the pot for the day. This only amounts to a few hundred dollars. However, after he takes out the entry fee, he only breaks even. If he loses the tournament, he's already lost money because he's had to pay his travel fees to the tournaments.

Ian was 39 years old and had started training for many different careers, but never completed any of them. He got his G.E.D. and tried to find himself. He told me he wanted to be a nurse, a math teacher, and a truck driver. He started taking classes but dropped out. I think he lacked the discipline to finish anything.

He was good at playing pool and pleasing the ladies in bed. Those were his real talents. However, this was not enough to support his two children or himself. As a result, he lived off of women in exchange for sex for many years. When they kick him out, he goes home to his mother until he charms the next woman into letting him move in with her.

After learning all of this, I knew I should have told him I was not interested and left him alone. He sweet talked me and we slept together after the third date. He was a great lover and I saw why women fell under his spell. I am divorced and have four children. Unlike Ian, my ex-husband pays child support. I'm a pre-school teacher and don't get out much.

A couple of weeks later, I let Ian move in with me and my kids. I assumed he would help out with the children and around the house. Wrong! He never got up to help me get the kids off to school and he used my car while I went to work. He didn't even try to help with homework or make any meals. He told me his only job was to please me in bed.

This sounds foolish now, but at the time, I was so lonely and just wanted a man around. My plan was to make this a "temporary" arrangement. Well, temporary turned into 10 months. My grocery bill doubled because all he did was eat when he wasn't in the bed with me. I turned into his maid because he didn't even pick up behind himself.

In the 10 months we lived together, he did not send one check to his baby mommas. He didn't even call the children and they couldn't call him because he had a prepaid Go Phone and didn't keep any minutes on it. This was because his hustling money was inconsistent.

I decided to kick him out. He was a terrible role model for my sons. Then I got the surprise of my life, I was pregnant with Ian's child. Even though I wasn't planning on more children, I decided to keep my child. I sat him down for a real "come to Jesus" conversation. He told me something I guess I already knew. He said, "I don't work because I don't want to pay child support." Once those words came out of his mouth, I knew it was over. I kicked him out and prepared to raise this child alone. If he never provided for the first two, I know he's not going to provide for this one.

However, I'm not like the other baby mommas. IF he ever gets a job, I will get child support whether he likes it or not.

### *Erica age 38 from Little Rock, Arkansas*

I met Michael at a surprise birthday party. He was a police officer. He was built like a body builder and all I could say was "Wow!" We began dating and I started asking about his family. He had five children by three different women. He was 40 years old.

After about three months of dating, I asked to meet his children. I had one son who was 12 years old. I was having a barbecue and thought it would be fun. He told me that they couldn't come because they had no way to get here. I expected him to pick up his children and since it was on a Saturday, his off day, it didn't make sense to me. They were ages seven, nine, ten, twelve and thirteen and lived in different parts of town. He said all of the mothers were jealous of each other and he just tried to stay out of the way. This was not the response I expected from a responsible father. A Red Flag!

Michael was a police detective and made a good salary. He had a beautiful home and drove a new Toyota Avalon and had a new motorcycle. I never saw any signs of his children at his home. He had four bedrooms and all of them were filled with "man cave" stuff. He had two daughters, but you couldn't tell by looking at the place.

A few weeks later, I asked about the children again. You see, I am a fourth grade teacher and love children. I thought we were close enough for me to ask if he paid child support. BIG MISTAKE! He nearly bit my head off! I just said "I thought it was strange that you never talk about them or see them. Perhaps the mothers' were not cooperating. Usually, that's because the father is not paying child support."

This is when he admitted that he didn't get along with the mothers and rarely saw his children. Two of the mothers tried to take him to court to initiate child support payments. However, he intimidated them and they didn't show up. He had a couple of his cop friends pay them a visit and advised that it wouldn't be wise for them to show up. Red flag number two! He pays them something when and if he feels like it.

He begged and begged me to have a child with him. For a brief moment, I was considering it. I called my best friend who is like a sister to me. She knocked some sense back into my head. She said to me "What makes you think he's going to support a child by you when he already has five kids waiting in line? Also, if the women gain the courage to fight him in court, how much will be left for your child? He or she will get 1/6 of the pie. "

I told Michael that I was not willing to have a child with him. He never talked about being exclusive or getting engaged. All he wanted was another child to brag about, but not support. If I was younger, I would have fallen into his trap.

Michael stopped calling after I gave him my decision. I know I dodged a bullet. Thank God! The last thing I need is a deadbeat dad in my life with baby momma drama.

# How To See The Truth

The truth is this is a selfish man and he doesn't care about taking care of his responsibilities. What women find attractive with this type of man is a mystery to me. I don't give these men any credit or respect because their children are suffering because of their lack of financial and emotional support. The children's welfare must come before anyone or anything. Period.

# Regain Your Standards

There is no excuse for a man or woman not supporting their children. They deserve nothing less. They became your responsibility the day they were born.

If you are dating a man that doesn't support his children, what would make you think he will support any children you might have together? Don't waste any more of your time or energy with him. Responsible men love and support their children financially and emotionally.

If you are married to him, ask yourself why are you allowing this? Why should the kids suffer if their father is able to work and provide, but chooses not to? If you continue to support a man that doesn't support his children, you are part of the problem, not part of the solution. This is a selfish and irresponsible man.

# Where Are Your Standards?

## Chapter Twenty

# HOW TO BECOME A DIVA WITH STANDARDS OR PRINCESS WITH STANDARDS

A Princess with Standards is an unmarried lady under the age of 25. A Diva with Standards is a lady 25 years and older, married or single. She doesn't tolerate unacceptable behavior from anyone. This is not limited to a boyfriend or husband. It includes your other family members, even your parents, siblings, nieces, and nephews.

You are in control of your life and body. Contrary to public opinion, you don't have to make numerous bad decisions in your teens and twenties or throughout your life. You can learn from others' mistakes. You don't have to be a statistic!

**Here's how to become a Diva or Princess with Standards!**

- Respect yourself at all times.
- Don't date married men or men that live with their girlfriends.
- Don't financially support a grown man. If he is able bodied and still won't work, that is his problem, not yours.
- Don't have unprotected sex with a man that is not your husband. You are not only protecting yourself from unplanned pregnancies, but also from sexually transmitted diseases, HIV or AIDS.
- Don't date or marry a man with no verifiable source of income. In other words, does he file state and federal income taxes each year?
- Don't date or marry a man with no work ethic.

- Stop living with a man you are not married to. You are providing all of the duties of a wife with no benefits. Girlfriends are not eligible for health and dental coverage under their boyfriend's policy. You must be related by blood or marriage.
- If you want to move out of your parents' home and can't afford it, get a couple of roommates and share expenses in an apartment.
- Don't use your body to get men to do things for you or buy things for you. This always turns out bad. If you want something, save up for it and buy it yourself. Remember rule number 1? Respect yourself at all times.
- Finish your education and pursue your passions. Since you must work to support yourself, why not do something you love?
- Do not buy property with a man you are not married to. This includes cars and real estate.
- Don't have children out of wedlock. If you already have a child, don't have any more until you are married.
- Don't date or marry a man that doesn't support his children.
- Don't date or marry a man with a "complicated occupation."
- Establish a savings account and put money into it every month.
- Don't ever agree to be a Back Door Girl. Remember rule number 1? Respect yourself at all times.
- Do your homework! Is he irresponsible or abusive in any way? If so, don't date or marry him. Remember, you are not meeting him, you are meeting his sales representative. You can't change him, fix him or cure him! Understand this from day one, you have a right to know who you are dating. Ask the key questions early in the relationship.
- Wear your dating button and evaluate each date going forward. I explain how to do this in my first book entitled *"Center of Attention"* available at Amazon.com and during my

workshops on healthy relationships. This is how you will discover if he is your boo or your boo-boo!

Chapter Twenty-One

# CONCLUSION

Life is about a series of choices. Sometimes you make good choices and sometimes you don't. I hope you make more good choices than bad. The good news is, if you make a bad choice, you can make another better choice to correct it. You don't have to remain in a bad situation. Don't beat yourself up. Everybody makes mistakes. I hope you learned from your mistakes so you don't have to continue to have bad experiences and memories your whole life.

Some of the stories involve men in multiple categories. For instance, you read about a man with a substance abuse problem with several ex-wives and a man who was abusive and lived with his girlfriend. The book is written so it would be easy to identify what you are dealing with. Once you know the truth, you have to face it head on if you want to establish and implement changes.

Only you can determine the standards for your life. You can see from the stories contained in the book what happens when you don't have any standards. You are like a wounded animal in the wild. All of the animals prey on you and devour you.

Respect is the one standard that is mandatory in every relationship and marriage. Respect, as you recall is a feeling of deep admiration for someone. It is the behavior demonstrated in front of someone in authority. Perhaps it is your parents, police officers, judges, religious leaders, etc. If he treats you with respect in front of them, why is it acceptable to disrespect you in private? Aren't you the same person with the same standards?

When you raise your standards, you become stronger and wiser. You learn the difference between a boo and a boo-boo!

You are not only required to establish standards, you must enforce them! Where are the standards for your life?

Become a Diva with Standards or a Princess with Standards today!

# www.ClassyDebra.com

www.ingramcontent.com/pod-product-compliance
Lightning Source LLC
Chambersburg PA
CBHW071438260626
47170CB00008B/2768